WE ARE GIANTS

AMBER LEE DODD

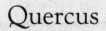

Quercus

QUERCUS CHILDREN'S BOOKS

First published in Great Britain in 2016 by Hodder and Stoughton

1 3 5 7 9 10 8 6 4 2

A CIP catalogue record for this book
is available from the British Library.

978 1 78429 421 2

Printed and bound in Great Britain
by Clays Ltd, St Ives plc

The paper and board used in this book are
made from wood from responsible sources.

Quercus Children's Books
An imprint of
Hachette Children's Group
Part of Hodder and Stoughton
Carmelite House
50 Victoria Embankment
London EC4Y 0DZ

An Hachette UK Company
www.hachette.co.uk

www.hachettechildrens.co.uk

For Gran, who would have liked this book

One

Have you ever tried to shrink yourself? You would be surprised at how easy it is. You just have to have a routine, be determined and, most importantly, keep it a secret. The only person who knows about it, apart from me of course, is my big sister, Jade. She was the one who helped teach me, although frankly I think she made half of it up. Once she told me I had to eat nothing but cat food. I was only six so I believed her. I stank so badly of cod chunks in jelly people started calling me 'Whiskers'. I did it for a whole week of school lunches before I realized she was having me on.

That's the problem with Jade – she's surprisingly good at making stuff up. It's not like I can check to see if what she's telling me is the truth, because she learned all the shrinking techniques from Dad. He died when I was five and Jade was nine. Dad didn't tell Jade about shrinking until he had to start going to hospital, and by then me and Jade had spent a lot of time growing. Still, I'm nearly nine and a half years old now but only as tall as a Year Four. A small Year Four at that. I would probably be a lot smaller if I remembered my shrinking routine more often. But, just like with brushing my teeth, I tend to forget. I think Jade forgets too since she seems to have grown a lot lately and not just in the height department. Let's just say she no longer needs to stuff cotton wool down her bra. I catch Mum looking at her sometimes with a sad look on her face.

My mum doesn't need to worry about shrinking, as she grew to 124 centimetres then just stopped. Even I'm bigger than her, although not by much. My mum is so small she can only just reach the light switches in our house. That's why our house is not like other people's. It's filled with children's furniture: little chairs and tables and even baby-sized wardrobes. It's a real live dolls' house inside. So when we step outside it's like walking into a giant's world.

I hate going outside and I especially hate going shopping, because we always bump into trolls. *Trolls* is what me and Jade call average-height people. Well, not *all* average-height people, just the ones who stop and stare or shout stupid things. You wouldn't believe some of the stuff people come up with. There was this guy at Asda who asked which one of the seven dwarfs my mum was. Or this couple in a bookshop who kept following us and saying how adorable we all looked. Once someone even tried to pick my mum up! My sister always finds secret little ways to pay these people back. Like pouring a jar of curry sauce into the Asda guy's bag or telling the bookshop security guard the couple had been shoving books down their trousers. They were quite a fat couple too, so it took the security guard some time to search them thoroughly. My mum jokes that they only do it because they're jealous. While they kept growing and growing, she got to stay the same. Perfectly formed and at the perfect height. Big enough to reach the ice cream in Asda, small enough to eat the kids' meals at McDonald's. Not everyone agrees though.

When Mum was born it was a bit of a shock because my grandparents came from a line of boring people. I mean they were a perfectly average size and shape for adults. They had perfectly regular jobs and they came from a perfectly ordinary family. Except for my Great-Aunt Shelley who lives in New Mexico and never wears any clothes. Nothing special or extraordinary had ever happened to either of them. So no one expected my mum to be a dwarf. When the doctor saw my mum for the first time, even he was surprised. She had to be wrapped up in a blanket and rushed away. When my grandma finally got to see her, it was obvious she was different. All the family crowded around the little hospital bed to have a peep at her. My Uncle Andy leaned over and said, 'Oh, I'm so sorry,' and his wife shook her head sadly as if my mum was a terrible disappointment. But my grandma just went on looking at my mum and said, 'The only thing to be sorry about is you, Andy – you and that witch of a wife of yours.'

Grandma told me it wasn't much different when Jade was born. Everyone crowded around again, only this time they couldn't believe that my mum and dad, these two tiny people, had produced such a huge and very loud baby.

Jade was so big and Mum was so tired that she couldn't manage to hold her. So Dad held her and sang her Beatles songs and Jade finally fell quiet. That was the moment he knew Jade was going to be a musician just like him. Or so Jade says. When I came along no one was surprised about anything. I was just another boring average-sized baby and Dad wasn't even there. He was at home with Jade.

Sometimes I think I'm forgetting Dad. So I try to remember things about him, little things, like his blue cable-knit sweater or the smell of his lemony aftershave and how he was so little, even smaller than Mum, but he had these great big hands. Hands that were always moving when he told stories. Then again, I'm not sure if those are my memories or Jade's. She remembers Dad better than me. She used to tell me everything about him. Even all the stories he told her. My favourite one was about dwarfs and giants. It went something like this:

The first people to walk the earth were a giant family. Mum, Dad and a daughter giant, who all towered over the trees. They lived together for many happy years playing marbles with huge boulders and eating cow kebabs. But as the years wore on, only the daughter giant, whose name was Anouk, remained, and she was lonely. She longed for a husband and children of her own.

One day as she wandered across the continents she stumbled on a whole tribe of people. But they weren't people like her. They were tiny people – dwarfs – and they had been living for hundreds of years just on the other side of the world. Anouk was so happy to have found other people, even if they were tiny, that she ran over, arms outstretched. But the dwarfs were scared and fled. All but one.

This was Tomas. He had a dark beard and eyes of fire and he didn't run from anyone. After some time Tomas and the giant became inseparable. They both longed for children. But Anouk was always scared of stepping on Tomas or of rolling on him in her sleep. So she prayed and prayed that she too could be a dwarf. And Tomas prayed and prayed he could be a giant. One day God answered their prayers and stretched little Tomas and shrank giant Anouk until they were average-size human beings. This is why people are the height they are today.

I used to imagine what it would be like, living

on the other side of the world where everyone was small. I thought it would be a lot like the Little People's Conference we went to once when I was very young. I don't remember much, apart from how happy Mum and Dad were and that being small felt really special. I could see why Dad wished me and Jade were like him and Mum. That's why he taught us the secrets to shrinking, so we could always be close.

We don't talk about Dad much any more, though I can tell Jade still misses him, even if she pretends she doesn't. I miss him too, or at least I think I do. Maybe I just miss the idea of him. Mum misses him the most. I think she sometimes gets lonely too. It must be so scary being the only little person in a world of giants.

Two

The day the shop closed down, Jade went to school like normal. But on the way home she dyed her hair pink. Actually, for the record, she said she didn't dye it pink, she *sprayed* it pink. I said I didn't think it mattered much, because either way Mum was going to flip out. Though I had to admit it looked pretty cool. Jade's got really long black hair, usually. But now that it was pink, it went with her earrings. Dangly electric-pink ones in the shape of thunderbolts. She's always wearing them, even though she's only meant to wear studs until Year Eleven and she's only thirteen and just started Year Nine. Jade never worries about these sorts of things.

I once had to wear trainers to school, instead of my black school shoes, and I spent the entire day trying to hide my feet. Which is surprisingly hard.

In almost everything, me and Jade are complete opposites. She has long smooth dark hair. I have thick reddish hair that's constantly falling over my brown eyes. She has big green ones. Her eyes are why she's named Jade, like the beautiful green stone.

I'm named Sydney, after the place I was conceived in. Which is totally gross, and I wish Mum had never told me.

Jade takes after Dad and I take after Mum. Well, apart from the whole height thing. You wouldn't know we were sisters, and Jade sometimes pretends that we aren't even related. She's supposed to collect me from my school and walk me home. But when she turned up with her hair sprayed pink she ignored me nearly all the way home. Whenever I said anything she just chewed on the ends of her hair.

'Don't give me that worried look,' she said as we turned the corner before the shop where we lived. 'The pink washes out, and nobody at school ever cares about the earrings.'

I just nodded.

'Don't you think it looks good?' she said, flipping her hair in my face.

'It looks great,' I said, and I meant it. But secretly I was worrying about how much trouble it was going to get her into.

'I went to the supermarket before I came to get you,' explained Jade. 'And they had this hairspray by the counter and I thought, Why not?'

I nodded again, thinking this wasn't much of an explanation, but it was generally best to agree with Jade. In my mind, I could see a picture of Mum getting very, very angry. I swallowed hard and did a quick shrinking exercise to calm myself down. I did what Dad called the '*Bullfrog*'. I puffed myself up while visualizing an inflated balloon. Then I breathed out as I imagined the balloon being deflated. As I did this I squeezed all my muscles right down to my toes.

I felt a bit better until I saw the sign on our shop door was turned the wrong way. Our shop is a furniture shop, but not just any ordinary furniture shop. It sells custom-made furniture. Just like the stuff in our house. People order it from all over the country and even sometimes from abroad, because we make one-of-a-kind things. Like when a man wanted a miniature wardrobe in the shape of a heart for his wedding anniversary. Or when someone's grandma wanted a three bears table and chairs for their three grandchildren. Each chair was a little smaller than the last because they were aged eight, five and two. Mum was so happy with this that she made our very own table and chair set, with the big chair for Jade, the middle-sized chair for Mum and the small chair for me. Although now I've swapped chairs with Mum, because I'm no longer the smallest.

Mum makes most of the special children's furniture, but her assistant Mandy, or Handy Mandy as we call her, helps Mum put together the bigger stuff as Mum finds it hard doing all the lifting. They make all kinds of amazing things together. They made a full-sized chair once, only it was covered in feathers and could be suspended from the ceiling. That was made especially for a posh fashion magazine, and supermodels were photographed in it wearing leopard-print swimsuits.

The shop was always open, even if there was no

one inside. There was always someone banging away in the back room, and usually when we came home we could see Mum from outside, sitting at the counter that's made from an old piano. But that day the lights were off and the sign said 'Closed'.

Jade squinted through the window and mouthed something, but I couldn't make out what. I wondered if she was doing a quick shrinking exercise too. She tried the handle and it was locked. We lived in a flat over the shop. We both had a key to the shop, but we never remembered them, because we never needed them.

'Mum!!!' we both shouted up to the window of the flat. Nobody answered. We waited a few minutes, then Jade decided we should pop into Miss Peters' shop. Miss Peters is about sixty and wears bright red lippy and a different scarf every day, even in summer. Her shop sells things that nobody really needs. Like egg timers in the shape of armadillos, vintage feather boas, paperweights in the shape of boobs and ice-cube trays in the shape of, well, you can guess.

Miss Peters looked up at us from a self-help book she was reading.

'Hello, you two,' she said. 'What are you doing here?'

'Mum's not in and we've no key,' I said.

'Ah yes, I think your mum may have nipped to the bank.'

'The bank? Is something wrong?' Jade said, looking up from an ice-cube tray.

'Well, no, I shouldn't think so. It's just been a bit slow for us all around here, and rents aren't getting any cheaper. But I shouldn't worry, pet. Your mum's shop has been around a long time.'

'Do you know when she'll be back?' I said, flopping back on to a tortoise-shaped beanbag.

'Shouldn't be too long, and you're welcome to wait here. You can even make yourself useful and try and sell some trinkets.'

So for the next hour and a half, me and Jade recommended things for people to buy. Jade was much better at it than I was. She sold a biker guy a lava lamp. Then she convinced a gang of women to buy six ice trays and a bunch of lollipops in the shape of, well, you-know-whats, for their hen party. Then she persuaded a toddler that her life would be much better if she had the beanbag in the shape of a tortoise. The toddler, after much crying, convinced her parents of the same thing. I managed to sell some bunny ears to the hen party and a dreamcatcher to the biker guy. I was sorry to see the dreamcatcher go, as I quite fancied it myself.

As the hen party left giggling, we heard Mum's truck grumble up the road. She's not a very good driver, even though the truck has special pedals. They fit over the accelerator and brake so Mum's legs can reach them. Mum always blames them for her driving, but Dad was little too and he was a brilliant driver. The truck stopped just short of the lamp post outside our shop. Mum climbed out and spotted us through Miss Peters' window. I noticed Miss Peters looking down anxiously as Mum came in.

'Sorry, Andrea – have they been getting in the way?' Mum said, brushing the beaded curtain from her face.

'Not at all – they've been selling all my stock. I haven't even been able to finish this chapter on "finding a man by not wanting a man" with all the trade they've been getting. How did it go at the bank?'

'I'll tell you later,' Mum said, sighing.

Once we were back in the flat, Mum poured herself a large glass of wine. She didn't ask us about our day. She didn't turn the telly on. She didn't even say anything about Jade's hair. I don't think she even noticed it.

'I'm just going for a little lie-down, girls,' Mum said, finishing her glass of wine. She clicked the bedroom door behind her. After a few moments we heard a snuffling sound.

'I guess she doesn't mind the hair,' Jade said jokingly, lying stiff on our mini purple velvet couch. She threw me a worried glance, flicked *Hollyoaks* on and turned the volume up. I stared at Mum's bedroom door, wishing I could see through it.

'I'm sure everything's all right,' Jade said.

I nodded and chewed my lip.

'Come 'ere,' Jade said, grabbing my arm and pulling me in close to her on the velvet sofa. I could tell she wanted to say something important, but *Hollyoaks* came back on. We ended up watching in silence as two characters on screen yelled at each other.

After *Hollyoaks* finished Mum came out in her

special pyjamas. They're part of a set. One pair in the set has gold stars on them and the other has blue crescent moons that glow in the dark. Since Mum and me were nearly the same size when she saw them, she got us a pair each. I have the moon ones and she has the stars. My pair were getting a little tight, even though I'm only taller than Mum when I stand up straight. I watched the stars on Mum's pyjamas glitter as she flopped down into the rocking chair. And I didn't know why, but my stomach suddenly felt as if it was full of those sharp little stars.

'Right,' Mum finally said, 'I think it's gonna have to be fish and chips tonight.'

Me and Jade looked at each other knowingly. Mr Wu, the owner of Lucky Fortune Fish, the chippy at the end of our road, doesn't wear trousers under his apron, just shorts. He says it's because of the heat of the fryers, but Jade reckons it's because he likes showing off his legs. Mum doesn't actually know about this because she can't see over the counter. But me and Jade have both had a glance at Mr Wu's knobbly knees.

That day he was wearing swimming shorts with

tropical fish on them. Jade sniggered and I went on tiptoes to get a better look.

'You have good look at my swimmer's legs?' Mr Wu said, shaking vinegar on to another customer's chips.

'Oi, mate!' the customer yelled. 'I said I didn't want no vinegar,' and he grabbed his bag of chips and rushed from the shop like his pants were on fire.

'So sorry, have a pickled egg, on the house,' Mr Wu called after him.

But the customer had stormed off before Mr Wu could unscrew the enormous jar of eggs on the counter.

'Three fish and chips with extra vinegar,' Jade said, slamming a ten-pound note on the counter.

'Two fish 'n' chips and one scampi 'n' chips,' I corrected her.

'OK, girlies,' said Mr Wu, 'but I have to microwave scampi – it's a special order. How's your mother? I've not seen her in a while.'

'Fine, thanks,' I replied.

'And how is the shop?'

'Fine,' Jade said in a strange, strangled voice.

'I hear you playing the guitar last night. You're getting good, Jade.'

My sister blushed. She doesn't like other people hearing her play. I don't know why, because she is really good. She's been playing since she was ten – that's when Mum gave her Dad's old guitar: a Fender Stratocaster. Sometimes I listen in when Jade's playing and imagine it's Dad.

'Right, girlies, here you are: very lucky fish and chips, also freshly made scampi.' Mr Wu plonked the grey-wrapped packages in front of us. Then he placed three fortune cookies on top.

'Special treats for beautiful girlies.'

The fortune cookies are the best thing about Lucky Fortune Fish. I suppose it pretty much makes up for Mr Wu's lack of trousers.

Mum looked a bit teary when we got back. But she rubbed her eyes and quickly poured another glass of wine. We ate our supper and watched an old film about a witch who runs a shop and falls in love with her neighbour. Mum loves these films because she thinks the sets are so beautiful. I secretly like them because you get to hear what the characters are thinking most of the time. Jade wasn't really interested, but she sat quietly and didn't make too many sarky comments. After it finished, Mum let out a big sigh.

'Mum, is everything OK?' I asked.

Jade and Mum looked at each other like they had been sharing a secret.

'Sydney . . .' Mum sighed and pulled her pyjama top over her legs. 'I'm going to have to let the shop go.'

I mushed the end of a leftover chip hard into my plate.

'I just haven't been able to sell enough furniture to keep up with the rent. But I don't want you to worry. Grandma has recommended me for a job at her old workplace, and her friend's got a flat we can let near to her.'

I took a deep breath and tried to imagine all my bones turning to jelly and my body folding up into a small concertina person. A person so small that they can fold themselves up and fit between the cracks in the floorboards and fall away. But nothing happened and I just stayed where I was, staring at my feet.

Jade said quietly, 'But Grandma lives in Portsmouth.'

'We have to move, honey-bun,' Mum said, pulling me to her. Jade stared out of the window and bit down hard on her lower lip. I flicked my fringe over my eyes. I didn't want Mum to see me cry.

'Hey, just think, no more smelly old London. No more getting stuck between sweaty men on the tube. And Portsmouth's on the coast!' said Mum. 'We'll be minutes away from the seaside. We can make sandcastles and go swimming and eat fish and chips whenever we want.'

'We can eat fish and chips whenever we want here,' Jade said.

'We can't leave. My school's here, and my friends,' I said, thinking about Anna and Harriet and all the people in class 5B.

I did not want to leave my friends. We had been through everything together, and I expected us to be friends forever. As I lay there, trying not to let Mum see me cry, I thought of Harriet and her first few weeks as the new kid in our class. She didn't know who to sit with or do group work with until me and Anna became her friends.

'You'll make new ones,' Mum said, giving me a squeeze.

I shook my head.

'Hey, we are the Goodrow girls! There's nothing we can't do,' Mum said, reaching for Jade.

'Nothing except keep the shop,' Jade muttered under her breath.

Mum stopped reaching for Jade and we all fell silent for what felt like forever.

Eventually Mum said, 'I think it's fortune-cookie time.'

Mum got the three fortune cookies Mr Wu had given us. We always liked to open them together after we'd eaten our meal. She cracked one open and burst out laughing. 'Ah, so that's my problem,' she said, then showed us the message. It said: '*It's time to think bigger.*'

Then Jade broke her cookie open and read us her fortune. '*You must choose your own future.*' This made her smile too.

But mine wasn't so good. It read: '*Change brings growth.*' I thought of Dad's disapproving face and scrunched up the paper and threw it on to the fish and chip wrappers.

Three

Usually when Grandma comes to visit, we have to spend three days preparing. One day to tidy everything, another day baking and filling the fridge with healthy green stuff, so it looks as if we don't only eat fish and chips, and a third day picking out outfits. Mum usually wears her best vintage blue dress with the velvet collar and pearl buttons, I wear the puffy red dress Grandma got me for Christmas, which makes me look like a giant tomato, and Jade wears anything that's not black and doesn't have skulls on it. But that day no one bothered. Instead we were all lying about in T-shirts and pyjamas. It was as if we had sort of given up trying to impress Grandma. And since we knew she was only here to help us make plans to move, we couldn't wait for her to leave.

When Grandma arrived she looked her normal stylish self, all in black with her long glossy grey hair pinned back, a silk scarf tied tight round her neck and a silver swan brooch pinned to her top. Grandma definitely doesn't look like other grandmas — she's not cuddly or old-fashioned. She's tall and elegant. Mum always says she wished she looked more like her. Years ago, Mum showed me a big photo album with all these old pictures of Grandma when she was young in long flared dresses and big winged sunglasses. She looked just like the black-and-white movie stars we like to watch. Grandma has a flair for the dramatic too.

'I have been thinking what I should give you when I die,' she announced over dinner.

Mum just looked at us and rolled her eyes. 'Would you like some more cake, Mum?'

'It's quite good. Store-bought, I assume?' Grandma said, wiping the corner of her mouth with a tissue. 'I was intending on giving my sister the pearls, but I'm not sure nudists wear pearls. So perhaps they would be better going to you?'

'I really don't think I have any occasion to wear pearls at the moment.' I could tell by the way Mum was biting her lip that she was trying to keep her temper.

'Nonsense. The tax office is a very respectable place. Lots of nice young men too.'

'You thought my dentist was a nice young man.'

Our dentist is about a thousand years old. He has a wooden walking stick for his bad knee, a huge moustache and always gives me and Jade stickers of elephants doing funny dances. Even though even I am obviously way too old for stickers.

'He has a nice steady job, and young women like you need a little –' Grandma sighed – 'how should I say? Ah, companionship.'

'Eww, Grandma, please!' Jade said, clapping her hands over my ears. 'Our young ears are not prepared for talk of Mum's love life.'

'A pretty woman like you, Amy. I can't understand why there's no man in the picture.'

'All right, Mum, I think the kids have heard quite enough for tonight.'

But once Grandma gets going, nothing can stop her. She leaned in close to Mum and whispered in her ear, but not quiet enough so we couldn't hear.

'It's the nose, isn't it? You took after your father there. Now, you know I said I would pay for it to be fixed.'

Jade burst out laughing, coughing bits of chocolate cake all over my pyjamas.

'Laugh all you want, but you have my nose too,' Mum said, turning to Jade. Then Mum squished an enormous piece of cake into her mouth and chewed it really slowly, so it got all over her chin and crumbled down her front. I watched Grandma squirm and dab her own face protectively.

'More cake, Grandma?' I said, making Jade snigger into her hand.

Grandma sniffed, raising an eyebrow at Mum's chocolatey chin. 'What a treat it will be to have you move nearer to me.'

Jade stopped laughing. Mum swallowed the rest of her cake and suddenly I didn't feel so hungry any more.

'You're going to love Portsmouth – the sea air, the history, the navy. And it's what I've always said you've needed: a fresh start, for you and the girls.'

Jade jumped to her feet, flipping her plate over.

'We don't need a new start. We like it here, in our home. We're just fine without you.'

I could see her bottom lip quivering and I knew she was on the verge of throwing one of her fits. Grandma looked like she'd been slapped. Everyone fell quiet. I could feel a big argument coming on, like the sparkly feeling you get just as a storm starts, so I closed my eyes and waited. But nothing happened. Instead, when I opened my eyes, Mum was holding Jade's hand and Grandma's hand was on Mum's knee.

Finally Mum said, 'Maybe you and your sister had better get to bed then, so we can talk on our own.' I wondered if they were going to start arguing about Dad, like they usually did when they were alone. But both of them had gone unusually quiet.

Even though it was barely nine o'clock, Jade and me trudged off to our rooms. We couldn't bear to hear about leaving the shop, the shop that Mum and Dad had set up together. With the sign that Dad painted himself: 'Goodrows. Tiny furniture. Grand Designs.'

Even Grandma used to like our shop. She used

to call Mum and Dad '*small* business owners', and tell everyone who would listen that Mum had her own shop. But when she found out that Mum and Dad couldn't afford to send us to posh schools, or buy a proper house, she started saying all these rude things about Dad. But we didn't need to go to posh schools with stupid school mottoes and shiny crests with dragons, lions and bears on. And we liked our flat. It had all our things in it, all our special places, like the kitchen door frame with our heights marked on it. It had been a long time since we had measured ourselves. The last time my height was under Mum's but right next to Dad's silver pencil mark. I used to go and touch it sometimes for luck, and try to remember something about him, like the way Jade said he used to laugh, beginning soft like music, until it got louder and louder like a motor starting up and everyone was laughing with him.

I like to think of Dad's laugh when I do my shrinking exercises. Especially when I do the special stretches. There are about twenty different ones that help shrink all the different parts of your body. Dad had names for all of them. My favourite is the '*Snake that Eats Itself*', where you have to start out as flat as a board and let all your muscles from your head to your toes go limp, like you're sinking into the floor, before, with a deep breath, you pull all your limbs towards your belly, till you're pulled in tight like a ball. If you want to stay as small and as special as my parents, you have to get your body used to shrinking up, have to teach your muscles how to fold up small.

Sometimes I imagine Dad doing these with Jade, doing these together in our flat, in our flat that we can't leave. We can't leave all our memories and all our secret places, like the spot under our bathroom sink where Jade used to leave scribbled notes for me until I wasn't afraid to go to the toilet in the dark any more. Or the roof outside Jade's window that's just big enough for us to both squeeze on to. Or the loose tile in the kitchen where every Easter Mum hides mini-eggs and sugared almonds for us.

As I tried to go to sleep, I thought of what Mum would be like as a boring office mum. All grey and serious and never home, just like Harriet's mum. Harriet has little packets of frozen food labelled with the days of the week to put into the micro-wave for dinner if her mum's working late. Then I thought about telling my friends how we had to move and how far-off Anna's voice already sounded when she said they would come and visit.

I climbed out of bed and knocked on Jade's door. I heard muffled sounds and opened the door to see her sitting on the roof, her legs out over the side. She didn't turn round when I squeezed myself next to her. My pale legs dangled next to hers and I gave her a gentle kick. Jade's foot nudged me back.

'Anna and Harriet said they are going to think of a plan to help us stay,' I said.

'Oh, well, now I know Anna and Harriet are on the case, I can relax.'

We went on swinging our legs into each other's, listening to the roar of cars in the distance.

'Jade, do you think . . .?' I paused, trying to find the right words. 'Do you think we might forget things if we're not here to be reminded of them?'

But Jade didn't answer; she just let her legs go limp.

I looked out over the London sky, over the city lights and out into the starless purple. I closed my eyes and felt very, very far away, as if I was a balloon floating up and up into the night sky. And I felt I might never find my way back home again.

Four

Anna and Harriet were not the best at coming up with plans. One time when we planned to get out of PE, we all said we had forgotten our school kit. But instead of getting to sit on the side and give each other tattoos with coloured pens, we had to wear the spare PE kit. The spare kit is pretty much the worst thing ever. It's a bunch of mismatched old tops and shorts that have been left behind by kids in the changing room. It's mostly boys' stuff and it smells like old socks, even though they say it's been washed. Harriet was convinced it hadn't been; she found mysterious grey stains all over her shorts and a nametag with Gary Phelps scribbled on it. So sometimes me and Anna call her Gary, when she's being bossy or hogging all the art stuff.

Art's my favourite lesson. I love to mix all the paints together or make collages. There's a corridor outside, where Mrs Mitchell hangs all the best artwork. Mrs Mitchell is kind of great, even if she was a little scary at first. She has messy hair, a loud voice and takes really long pauses so you never know when you can stop listening. She made it a special mission to learn three facts about each of us. She knew that:

1. My mum is a little person. (That's pretty obvious though, so she said it didn't count as one of my three things.)
2. Art is my favourite subject, followed by history.
3. I am the only girl in my class who doesn't mind picking up the frogs and toads in the environmental area next to the playground. I don't mind that they are a bit slimy. They look cute with their big eyes and I like to feel them breathing inside my hands.
4. I always go to the loo with Harriet and Anna, and sometimes they come in with me and put their feet up against the cubicle wall

so no one can tell. (Mrs Mitchell tells us off about this all the time because we leave scuff marks on the wall.)

Mrs Mitchell also loves to decorate the classroom to match whatever topics we're doing. At the moment the room is decorated like ancient Egypt, which we've been studying in history, so there are gold hieroglyphics on the walls and paper pyramids suspended from the ceiling.

We were painting sarcophaguses the day I told them about moving to Portsmouth. Anna isn't very good at art, so she was messing about a bit with the art supplies and ended up covered in gold glitter. Harriet had spent all lesson being very quiet and thoughtful. Finally she turned to me and said, 'I've been thinking that we should capture you.'

'Capture Sydney? How?' Anna asked.

I thought about a shadowy figure snatching me in the dead of night. I added more gold paint to my Egyptian mummy, which was coming out all wobbly and looking more like a ghost. Usually I was top of the class in arty things, but I hadn't been able to concentrate. Everything I tried to draw came out too big and blobby. Mrs Mitchell smiled at me and said, 'Very nice, Sydney.' But I knew she was just saying it to make me feel better, because she didn't offer to hang my artwork up in the corridor.

'No, no, we'll just make it *look* like she's been kidnapped,' Harriet continued.

'Oh, right,' Anna said, as she applied a layer of glue to her hand. 'Why would we do that?'

'Well, we make it look like she's been kidnapped. But secretly we hide her. You get it now?'

Anna nodded, but she didn't look too certain and I didn't feel too certain either.

'You can hide at my house,' said Harriet, with a look on her face like when Mrs Mitchell tries to explain long division to the boys at the back of the class. 'My mum's never home in the day, so you could have the whole house. And at night you could sleep in the attic. We could put Anna's inflatable couch up there for you to sleep on, and I have an old night light shaped like a bunny that you could have.' She looked at Anna. 'And if you stayed over, we could take turns sneaking food and stuff up to Sydney at night.'

'Oh, Sydney!' Anna squealed. 'You could be our secret friend.' And with that she peeled off the last of the glue from her hand with a satisfied little sigh.

I had a lot of questions, like, what would I do about school? Would I just sit in Harriet's attic getting older and older and stupider and stupider, until I was this shrivelled-up grey old woman who still couldn't do her seven times table and only knew about ancient Egyptian burials and bits of World War Two? Would I forget all the planets in the solar system and all the star constellations me and Mum had made up?

But Harriet has a way of convincing you any idea of hers is good. Like the time we decided to make our own ice-cream flavours and Harriet mixed pickles into strawberry swirl and then made us each try some. That was a proper 'Gary' moment. I haven't been able to touch strawberry ice cream since.

Harriet was so excited about her idea that when we went back to her mum's house after school she started cutting up letters from old magazines for the ransom note.

'We have to have a note to prove you've been

kidnapped,' she said, as if it was the most obvious thing ever.

I could see Jade taking one look at our ransom note, with its glossy teen magazine letters, and knowing we'd made it. But I didn't say anything because we all knew, despite the cool den Harriet had promised to make in her attic for me and Anna's promises to fetch me Crème Eggs and pickled onion Monster Munch every day after school for my midnight snacks, it was never going to happen. Sometimes though it's nice to pretend, even if it's just for a little while. It was nice to believe I wouldn't have to leave Anna and Harriet. I wouldn't have to leave London, or my school, or everyone I know. And I knew Anna knew it was pretend too, because she kept leaning over and nudging me and not saying anything.

Harriet looked up from sticking down the million-pound demand in bold pink letters on the ransom note. 'Come on, you two – let's go make that den,' she said.

Harriet's attic is more like a crawl space dripping with silky cobwebs. We had to move around on our hands and knees through the dust and use Harriet's rabbit-shaped night light as a torch.

When we had reached the tallest part at the back, Harriet found a little pop-up tent. It took all three of us, crouching and banging our heads, to open it out. Then Harriet went to get snacks.

By the time she came back with her arms full of tortilla chips and minty biscuits, Anna and me had wrestled the tent into the corner and made it lie flat. We were covered in dust and cobwebs and our backs ached from not being able to stand all the way up, but we were feeling pretty pleased with ourselves for defeating the terrible tent monster.

'No, not there,' said Harriet. 'Don't put it there. It needs to be more to the side, so there's room to get in and out.'

Me and Anna looked at each other and each raised one of our eyebrows. Then we turned to Harriet and yelled, 'Shut up, Gary!'

Then we fell about in fits of laughter.

I felt a bit like crying afterwards though, so once we had all rolled into the pop-up tent Harriet and Anna squeezed up to me and wrapped their arms around me to make a friend-sandwich.

In the glow of the bunny night light I wondered if I would ever find friends like these again.

Five

The next few weeks went by in a daze. As all the other shops started putting up Valentine's decorations, Mum and Jade started packing the stuff from our shop into boxes. They argued about who was packing what. Or how they should pack it. Or who should make the tea. They argued about everything.

Just before half-term Anna and Harriet gave me a huge card and a going-away present. It was a big gold notebook with swirly patterns on the edges. I wanted to give it back to them to tell them it was all a joke, that I wasn't leaving school, that I wasn't leaving London and most importantly that Mum wasn't losing the shop. But I didn't, I just took the notebook.

'It's so you can write down the exciting stuff

you get up to,' Anna said, while Harriet stared at her shoes.

But I did not want exciting stuff to happen. I wanted the same things to happen. I wanted to help out at Miss Peters' shop and buy pickled eggs from Mr Wu. I wanted to walk back to the shop every day with Jade and see Mum behind the piano counter.

When me and Jade got home the day before we were due to leave, Mum was putting the last of our things from the flat into boxes. I was surprised to find that Mr Wu had come by to help with the packing. I was glad to see he was wearing trousers, but he'd never come to our home before.

'Hello, honey-bun,' said Mum. 'Miss Peters and her friend have offered to help with the packing. Isn't that kind?'

I could see that Miss Peters wasn't really help-ing. She was sitting on a box drinking a glass of wine, swinging her feet back and forth and look-ing at Mr Wu.

'What am I going to do without you, Amy?' Miss Peters said, hiccupping.

'I'm afraid you'll have to go to the singles salsa

classes without me,' Mum said, taping up a box that had 'kitchen stuff' written on the side.

'I guess you could come with me,' Miss Peters said, leaning towards Mr Wu. 'You've certainly got the legs for it.'

'Jade, can you help, please?' said Mum. 'Hey, Mr Wu, don't stack them so high. I won't be able to reach that.'

'So sorry,' he said, but I could tell he wasn't concentrating. 'Yes, I'd love to dance with you sometime,' he said to Miss Peters.

'Is there anything I can do?' I asked, throwing my school bag into the smallest of the three bear chairs.

'I think we're all done in here, Sydney,' Mum said, taking a step back.

Everyone stopped for a moment to look around the bare flat. Me and Jade got a bit teary and Miss Peters stopped swinging her legs.

'I brought you some goodbye gifts,' Miss Peters said, reaching into a large bag. 'One for each of you.'

She passed me a wooden box. Inside it there were three trays — two of different types of paints and brushes and the third one with special artist pencils and pens. It was so lovely I could barely say anything, and I only just managed to squeeze out a small 'thank you'.

'You are welcome, dear. It is so you will always have art in your life,' Miss Peters said. 'And this is for you, Jade,' she went on, pulling out a small black box from behind her chair.

'Oh, wow!' Jade cried out. 'A portable amp!'

'So you will always have music,' Miss Peters said. Then she stood up and reached around for what she had been sitting on. It looked like a dead dog wrapped in tissue paper. 'This is for you,' she said to Mum.

Mum unwrapped the package to reveal a fur coat.

'How lovely,' said Mr Wu.

'I saw it the other day,' gushed Miss Peters, 'and thought it would look marvellous on you. See, it's your size – petite.'

'It is lovely,' Mum said, 'but I'm not sure if I—'

'Darling,' Miss Peters interrupted, 'if anyone could wear this, it's you.'

Mum smiled politely. Then Mr Wu stepped

towards her and gave her a carrier bag. When Mum reached inside she found three paperback romance novels.

'So you always have romance,' said Mr Wu, but he wasn't looking at Mum when he said it.

Mum held up the books so we could see the covers. One had a picture of a pirate holding a swooning woman. Jade snorted with laughter.

'Hush, Jade,' said Mum.

'I like them,' I said, and everybody smiled at me.

And it was true. I did like them. They were the kind of books I like. Not to read of course. Yuk! To do my shrinking with. They're the right size and shape and they're all paperbacks. The perfect kind of book to balance on my head. If I can balance enough books on my head, it stops me growing. So far, I can balance four books when I'm standing up and five when I'm sitting very still. Dad could balance ten, and not just paperbacks. Once he balanced an encyclopaedia.

Mr Wu cleared his throat. 'I have also brought some fortune cookies,' he said, and then he handed me a massive paper bag with more cookies than I could count. 'I guess they can help you figure out the future. Or just provide you with something to nibble on the journey to Portsmouth,' he said.

'Thank you, thank you, both,' Mum said. 'I'm really going to miss you.'

'Who's this?' Jade asked, pointing at the door. Someone was twisting a key in the front door lock. Then Mr Hadlow, the landlord, appeared.

Miss Peters sighed. 'I guess we'd better be going then.' She bent down and gave Mum a kiss on each cheek. Mr Wu raised his eyebrows at Mr Hadlow, who was wiping a finger over the curtains.

'Goodbye and good luck,' Miss Peters said, linking arms with Mr Wu.

Mr Hadlow is one of those men who are completely bald apart from a few strands of hair. He combs these across his head. He stood by the window and let out a little moan as he examined his dusty fingertips. 'I will never be able to rent this place out again like this,' he said to my mum. 'What have you done to it? It's much, much smaller.'

'It's exactly the same size it's always been,' Mum said, and she rolled her eyes at me. Mr Hadlow is always like this. Always nagging Mum about something. We hate the way he lets himself in on rent day. Mum has told him off about it loads of times. But we wouldn't have to put up with it much longer now.

'No, no, I distinctly remember it being bigger,' he said, turning to face us. 'Maybe it's because of the colour. You repainted?' he asked my mum.

'You know I did, Mr Hadlow,' said Mum. 'Just as you know I will put on a fresh coat of white paint before I leave. I *will* have my security deposit back, Mr Hadlow.'

'Hmm,' grunted Mr Hadlow. 'Make sure that you do. You made the place look smaller.'

'Is that all, Mr Hadlow? Because we still have a lot of packing to do and the flat is ours until Monday,' said Mum.

'I have to check,' said Mr Hadlow as he shuffled towards the open door. Then he mumbled, 'I knew I shouldn't have let people like you have this place.'

'What do you mean?' shouted Mum. 'People like who?'

She stood and faced him, her arms folded in

front of her chest. Me and Jade went and stood behind her. Our arms were folded too.

'I mean . . . I mean . . .' he stammered. 'I mean, decorators, furniture-makers, creative people. People who like to change things. I wasn't talking about midgets, I mean dwarfs, no, I mean little people. I'm sorry – what do you like to be called?' he said, patting the hair across his head.

Me and Jade waited for Mum to explode. She hates the word 'midget'. It's a truly horrible thing to say! I had to ball my hands into fists and Jade flushed red with anger. But Mum didn't yell, she went quiet, narrowed her eyes and held Mr Hadlow's gaze.

'I like to be called Amy,' said Mum. 'It's my name.'

'Yes, well, um, Amy, I'll, um, send you your deposit. Um, and remember to leave the keys.'

Mr Hadlow backed out of the flat so fast we heard him bang into the staircase banister below. It made me think of the first time Miss Peters had moved here. She had acted like a typical troll around Mum at first. She had been ever so polite but hadn't quite known what to say to Mum. She went quiet whenever we came in the shop and called Mum Mrs Goodrow. That was until Mum made her laugh with a dirty joke.

I wondered how long it would take for people in Portsmouth to get used to us. Or if they ever would.

Six

It only took two hours to take us away from our old life and bring us to Portsmouth. I thought it would take longer. Like the time we flew from London to Australia. It took us all day and all night. When we arrived everything was completely different. People talked in different voices, like they were asking questions all the time. And it was so hot. The heat made everything flicker before you, like it was about to catch on fire.

It wasn't like that when we got to Portsmouth. It was another grey city, just like London really. People even had the same accent. And where we had to live we couldn't even glimpse the sea. The only thing that felt different was me. I felt like my insides had been flipped upside down. I tried to tell

Jade, but she had her headphones in the whole time we were moving.

Our new flat was on the fourth floor. We had to carry all our stuff up because Mum could only afford to pay the movers to unpack all the stuff from our furniture shop into a storage place over the hill. We passed it on the way and watched two removal men hump all the furniture from our shop into these sad little orange sheds. Thankfully the new flat was semi-furnished, so we didn't have to bring beds. Most of what we needed, Mum could fit in our truck. But even though the truck had five seats and a flatbed, we spent most of the journey crammed against boxes. And by the time we'd carried half the stuff up to our new place, Mum was exhausted. She only has little legs, so it's much harder for her to carry things up four flights of stairs. She was pretty puffed out by the time we made our last trip, so Jade had taken Mum's hand and practically pulled her up the stairs. Just our luck though, because our new neighbour's little girl popped out and saw.

'Mummm!' she screamed. 'Look at it, look at it.' But her mum didn't come out; another girl about

Jade's age did. She didn't scream though. She got out her mobile phone and took a picture. I turned back and stared at her. I imagined my eyes becoming hot like lasers and my stare burning into her brain, turning it to mush. But the girl with the phone just stared back blankly. I waited for Mum to say something, to get angry, or even make a joke of it, but she didn't. She just sighed. It was like she didn't even have the energy to get upset.

She *was* upset about the flat though. She tried to hide it by giving us a great big smile. But it was one of those smiles that don't reach your eyes. It just stays on your lips while the rest of your face does something different.

'It's not too bad,' she said. 'We just need to see it with our own things in it.'

But when we finally unpacked we got to see the true horror of it. Off from the hallway were two bedrooms and across from our room was an open-plan kitchen and living room. The kitchen part was horrible. There was just a grimy old cooker, a fridge and a couple of cupboards pushed to the corner of the room. The bathroom at the end of the hallway was worse though. It had this ancient toilet with a chain. Jade dared me to use it first. I thought I'd just hang on for a while. Mum's room was one of those ridiculously tiny box rooms. It fit a bed and Mum and not much else. At least our room was not too bad. It had a window with a ledge outside to put flowers on. From the window, I could see a corner shop with a big England flag hanging over the door. And if I squinted, I could see the orange lock-ups on the hill, where what was left of the shop was. I almost wished we could have moved into them. Even those sheds looked better than our flat. But at least mine and Jade's room had enough space to fit in two single beds, Jade's guitar and my treasure chest.

My treasure chest is a big old trunk that Dad made. It looks like it belongs on a pirate ship, with a big brass lock and a heavy wooden lid. I used it for my best things: my new art box from Miss Peters, some perfume in a dinky glass bottle that Jade gave me and a soft white rabbit toy from Dad. I used to take the rabbit to bed but I'm too old now. I couldn't get rid of it though, so it lives in the box.

Looking around to check Jade had gone, I

chucked everything out of the chest and climbed in. To fit into it now I have to fold myself up. You have to do it a certain way. First you cross your arms over your chest and then you pull your legs up to your belly and tuck your chin in. Then you roll to one side. I've learned with practice to roll on to my side quick so the lid closes. I can stay like this for twenty minutes before I get cramp. The tricky bit is getting the lid open. It never shuts completely, but sometimes the hinges stick. I have to give it a proper bang to shake it open, which is hard when you're all folded up. I tried not to think about that and closed my eyes to focus on shrinking thoughts, but all I could think about was Dad. I remembered timing how long Dad could hold his breath. Once he convinced us that he could hold it for ten minutes. Of course he cheated. But I remember watching with a stopwatch in awe. I imagined Dad timing how long I could stay in the chest. And I almost wished the hinges would stick. Then I could stay in there forever. But I heard Jade coming, so I popped the lid and climbed out.

It was weird sharing a room with Jade. We

couldn't just talk to each other like normal. Sometimes we had to pretend we couldn't see one another, so when one of us got changed or wanted to read a book the other person wouldn't distract them. But it wasn't like I could read a book then anyway. I don't think Jade could play the guitar either.

We ended up getting into our pyjamas after dinner and turning off the light really early. But I couldn't go to sleep; my mind was all swirly.

'Jade, do you think everyone here's going to be like those girls?' I said, in the darkness.

Jade sniffed. 'They'll get used to us. People usually do.'

'Trolls,' I muttered.

'I wish you wouldn't call people that,' Jade said. 'We're not babies any more.'

We both fell quiet for a long time. I stared up at the ceiling and tried to imagine it was the sky, and that I was staring up at millions of stars instead of millions of white plaster bumps. I listened to Jade sigh and turn over. And suddenly I became terrified of being left awake alone in the darkness.

'Jade, what do you think Dad would have

thought of this place?' I whispered at the lump in Jade's bed.

'Mmmrrrr,' the lump murmured.

'Sometimes I worry I'm forgetting bits of him.'

Jade shifted and became an upright lump in the bed.

'Hey, I'm as tiny as an ant, I'm as tiny as a mouse,' Jade said, leaping out of bed and dragging me to my feet.

'Close your eyes and imagine yourself getting closer and closer to the ground,' she screamed as she took my wrists and spun us round.

'Don't let go now, cos we're getting smaller and smaller,' she said, before tripping over her feet and sending us tumbling to the floor.

'Feel any different?' she said, laughing.

Even though Jade hadn't got half the words right and she didn't take it very seriously, it felt good to do it with her again. I was like I could almost feel Dad doing it with us. Teaching Jade all the right steps.

'I haven't done that in years,' Jade said. Then she yawned and flopped back on to her bed.

I didn't like to tell her I still did it all the time.

Seven

Mum had to wear a suit. I'd never seen her in a suit before. It didn't look good. Mum usually wears children's clothes. She has all sorts of kids' T-shirts, some plain, some with prints on them. She even has a couple of Mickey Mouse ones that used to be Jade's. Sometimes Mum finds it hard to buy children's clothes though, because even though she's little she has the body of a woman, big boobs and all. Trousers are the worst though because her bum's a lot bigger than most kids'. So she's always nipping in the waist or letting them out with elastic and she has plenty of dresses. The rest of her things, like coats and gloves, she buys from vintage shops. People used to be a lot smaller in the old days, so a lot of the clothes have shorter arms and smaller shoulders. Mum turned this beautiful jacket from the 1940s that had pearl buttons and a fur collar into a coat. Miss Peters even found her some vintage leather gloves to go with it.

But children's clothes don't include business outfits, and suit trousers from second-hand shops usually smell like wee. So Mum had to buy an ordinary pair and cut the legs up. But it still looked awful. She looked even smaller than usual, swamped in these enormous grey trousers. She couldn't find a jacket to go with it, so she bought a waistcoat from the boys' section. It didn't look much better. It wasn't really meant for women. She looked all squashed in at the top and all baggy at the bottom.

'Well, now, don't you look a treat!' Grandma said when she arrived to look after me and Jade as it was half-term. 'Like a proper businesswoman, perfect for your first day.'

Grandma had helped Mum prepare for an interview for the tax office. Mum went for it the day after we arrived and came back looking sadder than when she left. Me and Jade were convinced she hadn't got the job, and that we would have to move in with Grandma. We'd all sleep on her pull-out couch, and get woken up at all hours of the night because Grandma wanted to check if we were still breathing, or if we needed any water, or just because she was a bit lonely and fancied a chat. Me and Jade were preparing ourselves to never sleep again when Mum told us she had got the job. She told us in a voice so small that we had to ask her to repeat herself three times. I still couldn't imagine it: Mum shuffling bits of paper around and looking at other people's bills. Mum doesn't even open the bills we get.

'Well, now, what a lovely place this is, Amy. So *petite*, so *mignon*.'

Whenever Grandma lies, she talks in French. Jade says Grandma has to do everything classy, even lying.

'Oh, and Sydney, it can't have been much more than a month, but my, how you have grown! *Très jolie*.'

I'm pretty sure I went a deep shade of beetroot and got my pouty-scrunchy face on, because Mum flashed Grandma a warning look.

I had grown? Not much, surely? With all the moving stuff we'd had to do and the sleepovers with Anna and Harriet, I had almost forgotten about my shrinking routine. I'd only managed to squeeze in a few exercises. After we left the shop, everything had changed so fast and I had started forgetting all of Dad's routines. I wondered if everything would keep changing until I forgot him altogether. Until I became just like Jade and shared nothing special with him and Mum any more. Dad would be so disappointed with me.

I scrunched up my eyes and tried to think of the story Dad told me about Alviss the master-craftsman dwarf, who made weapons for Thor, the god of thunder.

Alviss and all the dwarfs lived in a castle under the earth, near the molten lava of the world, where they forged weapons used by only dwarfs and gods. The dwarfs were strong and wise and were worshipped for their skill with metal. But they had one weakness: they could never go to the surface in the light of day or they would be turned to stone.

Alviss grew lonely, living so far beneath the ground. So, in exchange for his weaponry and wisdom, Thor promised him the hand of his daughter Trud when she was old enough to marry. When the time came, however, Thor couldn't bear to part with his daughter, so he set about to trick Alviss.

One night, Thor called Alviss to the surface and demanded that he prove his wisdom to make up for his short stature. Alviss, being quite offended by this, told Thor he was at least two inches taller than the average dwarf, but agreed to submit to Thor's challenges. Long into the night Thor challenged Alviss's cunning and at every task Alviss bested Thor. Thor knew he could never outsmart the master craftsman with ordinary tests and trials so he set him one more task, one more riddle.

'Tell me, Alviss, if you are so wise and so worthy of my daughter, how large is the sun?' Thor's voice echoed across the mountains.

'I've never seen the s-sun b-before, so how c-can I answer that?' Alviss stammered back. For the first time that night he was stumped.

'Well, little one, you will now!' Thor laughed and the world trembled and the sun rose from behind the mountains. Thor had been cunning and kept Alviss up the whole night solving riddles and problems.

Alviss realized too late that he had been tricked, and as

he twisted around to see the rising of the sun, he turned to stone.

But I couldn't remember what happened next: if Alviss managed to outsmart Thor or he stayed turned to stone forever. And Jade wouldn't tell me Dad's stories any more, not even secretly at night when we were both sad. Not since we moved away.

To make things worse, at the end of half-term I ran into the girls from downstairs again. The little one just giggled and slammed their door as I came down the stairs to pick up our post, but the older one was spread out across one of the bottom steps, her back against the banister, her feet up against the wall, leaving scuffy trainer marks, chatting loudly on her mobile.

'Yeah, yeah, I know he's well ugly, and I can say that because he's my cousin. I don't know how Becca could fancy him.'

I stood there waiting for her to move, but she just stretched out sideways on the stairs and continued talking fast into her mobile. I tried to shuffle round her, but I couldn't squeeze past and I was half afraid she might trip me as I went past.

So I gave up and was going back up when I heard her say, 'Oh my God, it's one of the neighbours I was telling you about. Yeah, yeah, it's getting well freaky in here.'

I wish I could have smacked her stupid troll face. If I had been Jade, I would have said something cool, or maybe even have given her the tiniest shove down the rest of the stairs. But instead I just thought of her head puffing up and up, her hands flapping by the sides of it as it got bigger and bigger. I imagined her nose being stretched right across her face, her eyes disappearing round the sides and then – pop. She would burst like a balloon.

I didn't tell Grandma any of this when she asked me for the thousandth time how I liked Portsmouth. Instead I said I liked watching the sailors go by in their uniforms and how I was looking forward to going swimming in the sea.

'Oh no, you can't actually go in the water. You have no idea what might be in it,' Grandma said.

'I'm going to swim in it naked,' Jade said. Then she stomped off to our new room.

Jade was doing a lot of stomping since we moved. Mum said the neighbours must think a herd of elephants had moved in. And I thought Grandma might have to start teaching me French, because I didn't dare tell Mum how much I hated Portsmouth.

Eight

Mum looked as sad and grey as her suit as she took me and Jade to school. It felt weird to be starting school after spring half-term in the middle of a week. Jade had to go to North Star secondary school. I had to go to Castle Cross primary. My uniform was all black with a black and red stripy tie. Jade had to wear a blazer, an actual blazer like schoolchildren from old books. She hated it. She couldn't get away with wearing her lightning-bolt earrings with it either. She could only wear studs. She had to wash out all the pink in her hair too. But I noticed she kept one strand pink. She pulled it back behind her ear and I saw that her studs were small silver skulls. Jade didn't stop playing with her strand of pink hair all the way to her new school. She looked around at the playground full of kids huddled in little groups before bolting out of the truck.

'I think our Jade is a bit on the nervous side, don't you?' said Mum, giving me a smile in the rear-view mirror.

'Mmm,' I muttered at my shoes, knowing my turn was next.

'I know it is going to be different, Sydney. But different doesn't have to be bad, you know.'

I couldn't think of one good thing about losing the shop and moving to the tiny flat with the mean girls. Going to a completely different place where nobody knew me and nobody knew Mum. I felt all sweaty and shaky. I closed my eyes and imagined myself shrinking. Shrinking away till I was almost invisible.

'Hey, you look pale. Are you feeling OK?'

I could have pretended I was ill. I'm excellent at fake-coughing. I could have had a coughing fit right then and there and Mum would have had to take me home. I could have been tucked under a blanket in the living room while Mum went to buy me the cherry-red cough sweets, the ones that give you the runs if you eat a whole packet. We could have watched rubbish daytime TV, where women talk about their wobbly bits and complain about their boyfriends. But it wouldn't have been the same. I couldn't just hang around in the back of the shop. Or be tucked up in bed with Mum checking on me every half-hour. I'd have to go back to the flat, and Mum would get in trouble for missing her proper job. Although I could tell she was hoping I was ill so she wouldn't have to go.

'I'm OK,' I managed to squeak. Mum looked at me sceptically as I tried to force a smile. 'I'm OK, really, Mum.'

'Do you want me to come in with you?'

I shook my head and clenched my fists together so Mum wouldn't see me shake, before climbing out of the truck.

'Knock 'em dead, honey-bun,' Mum yelled before pulling off, leaving me in the busy playground.

The playground was filled with noise. The screams of kids doing cartwheels. The *whoomp, whoomp* of a football being bounced hard against the school wall. The clamour of voices surrounding a blonde girl waving a new mobile phone around. Automatically I looked for Anna and

Harriet. I saw two girls on a bench swinging their legs, one with long blonde hair, the other with brown braids. It took me a few seconds to realize it couldn't be them and I suddenly missed them more than ever.

I remembered the yogurt fight we had in the playground once. It had started off an accident – as I peeled back the lid of my yogurt, some of it splashed Anna. So Anna had taken a spoon and flipped some at me, but it was a bigger spoonful than she had meant and it hit Harriet instead. Harriet had picked up her pot of chocolate mousse and chased me and Anna round half the playground. By the end of the break we were all covered in chocolate mousse and yogurt. It was even funny when we got told off. After that, whenever Harriet had chocolate mousse we got the giggles. I wondered what they were doing now and if they had found a new girl to replace me.

'Are you lost?' A boy's voice came out of nowhere.

'Sorry?' I said.

'Are you lost?' the boy said again. He looked like he was made out of puff pastry. He was very pale and very round with blue eyes that seemed to dart everywhere from beneath thick black curly hair. But he wasn't wearing the Castle Cross school jumper. Instead he was wearing a black cardigan.

'This is Castle Cross school, isn't it?' I asked, staring at his cardy, suddenly worried Mum had dropped me off at the wrong school.

The boy looked down at his cardigan. 'Yeah, course,' he said, then: 'I'm just wearing this cos I bust my school sweater.'

'Like Superman,' I said, imagining Clark Kent ripping through his shirt to reveal his Superman costume.

'Ha ha, I wish,' he said, wiping his hand on his cardigan before offering it to me to shake. 'I'm Bobby.'

'Sydney, after the capital of Australia,' I said, as he nearly shook my arm off.

'You could have been called Albion, you know.'

'What?'

'When Arthur Phillip founded the first settlement in Australia he was going to call it Albion. But he changed his mind and called it after the man who issued the charter allowing him to build it, Lord Sydney. That's lucky for you, cos Albion sounds like a wizard's name or something.'

'What? Who's Lord Sydney?'

'Oh, um, I haven't got that far on Wikipedia yet.'

'Wikipedia?'

'Yeah, you know, on the Internet. It's got facts on everything. You can even go on and write about things you know about. I'm on it so much, Dad thought I was looking at dodgy stuff. He'd prefer it if I was; be a bit more normal for a boy, he said . . .' Bobby said, trailing off and looking around the now empty playground. 'I'd better get to class,' he added.

'Wait, I don't know which class I'm in.'

'Oh yeah, you're new, aren't you?'

'How did you guess?' I said.

'People don't normally talk to me.' He looked down, scuffing his feet against the gravel. 'I'll take you to reception. They'll know what to do with you.'

'Is it all right here?' I asked, as we made our way to the double doors.

'Yeah, mostly, apart from if you get my teacher,

Mrs Pervis. She used to be all right, but then she got hit by the school minibus chasing a kid who was bunking class. Now she's a total loon.'

The lady at reception made me wait a long time while she fiddled with the Post-it notes on her computer. Finally she looked up at me through glasses pushed to the end of her nose. She looked a bit like an owl. I imagined her pecking at the glass that separated me from the reception area.

'Sydney Goodrow?'

I nodded.

'Alison – one of your classmates – will be along in a moment to show you around the school and settle you into your new class,' the owl woman said.

'Which class will I be in?' I asked nervously.

'You'll be in 5F with Mrs Pervis.'

Nine

It took Alison forever to arrive and take me to my doom. I sat waiting on a hard plastic chair, watching people swish back and forth through the electric doors. Most of the teachers pretended not to see me at all when they stopped for a moan with the receptionist. The receptionist flapped her arms as she got more and more involved in a rant. I couldn't help giggling at her, and a teacher turned to stare at me. Alison arrived just in time to rescue me. I recognized her as the girl with the mobile phone from the playground. She tilted her head and squinted her eyes at me.

'You must be the new girl,' she said. 'Come with me. I'll show you the dump.'

The school wasn't a dump, but it certainly wasn't like me and Mum had imagined. When we heard it was called Castle Cross, we had pictured suits of armour in the hallway – a really old-fashioned place where the girls had to wear straw boaters and curtsy all day long. But when I got inside, there were the same tatty healthy-eating posters on the walls you see in every school. The same grey carpets, the same smelly hall for PE and assemblies. Not a velvet curtain or suit of armour in sight.

Alison led me past rows of classrooms, all the while twisting the end of her ponytail.

'These are the classrooms,' she said, waving a limp arm. 'And this is the girls' loo,' she went on. 'There are two girls' loos, one upstairs and these ones. Don't use these though, cos the doors don't lock.'

'Alison, is Mrs Pervis a bit, um, well, nuts?' I asked as I searched for an escape window.

'Oh yeah, the rumours are totally true. She used to be all right until that Year Six set fire to her hair with a Bunsen burner. Now she can just flip out any time. So where you from?' she asked, as she led me up the staircase.

'London.'

'Ooh,' she said. 'Near Harrods?'

'Uh, no, not really. We lived in south London. Battersea.'

'But you must have gone there all the time, right?'

'Only once or twice with my dad, but I can't really remember what it's like.'

'Oh,' Alison said. 'This is our classroom.' She stopped outside the door. I looked through the window. No artwork, no posters, no masks and lanterns hanging from the ceiling like in my old classroom. Just rows of kids I didn't know.

Mrs Pervis was sitting at the end of her desk, moving her pointy heels back and forth.

As I followed Alison in, she glanced up and made a tick on her register. Then she carried on talking to the class. Alison slipped into her chair beside the girls I had thought were Harriet and Anna. But there wasn't a space there for me. I wandered past a few tables and tripped on someone's bag.

'Sydney, you may be new, but I'm sure your old school expected you to sit for lessons. So I suggest you stop distracting the class and find a seat,' Mrs Pervis snapped, looming over me.

I got up, brushing my knees, and I saw a big arm

71

at the back waving at me. An arm belonging to Bobby.

He moved over and I found a chair by him. But it was a bit of a squeeze because I was sitting on the end of the table. Mrs Pervis lifted a pencil-thin eyebrow as I tried to squish my feet under the desk.

'Today we will be doing our World War Two projects. I will be handing out topics for you to research and I expect you all to give a presentation at the end of the day. Now get into groups.'

I looked hopefully over at Alison and the two girls at the front. But they had all linked arms and had their heads together.

'Wanna be my partner?' Bobby asked.

'Um, OK,' I said, watching the classroom divide into threes and fours, leaving me and Bobby alone at the back.

Mrs Pervis handed out the topics as the other groups grabbed coloured paper and pens. We got a little grey card with the words 'WW2 survivors' on it. I groaned inwardly. Why, oh why hadn't I paid attention last half-term? We had been doing this topic at my old school, but I hadn't really been able to concentrate, even though I love history. I always try to imagine what I would be like if I'd grown up in a different time. When me and Jade were younger, we used to play all sorts of games set in the past. Our favourite was pretending we were Victorian ladies. We used to dress up in Mum's clothes and Mum would sometimes pretend to be our servant. She would fetch us tea and make us cucumber finger sandwiches for lunch. I had kind of lost interest in everything, even art, ever since the day Mum told us we had lost the shop. In the end, at my old school, I just stared out of the window or passed notes to Anna and Harriet under the desk. Notes that read, *I wish I didn't have to move to stupid Portsmouth.*

To which Harriet had replied, *'Don't go. You can stay in my attic and I'll feed you biscuits.'*

And Anna had drawn our three little faces. Her face had lots of dotty freckles, Harriet's had her tight little dreads and gold stud earrings and mine had a mass of crazy gingery hair and we were all holding stubby stick hands.

I imagined Anna drawing faces and stick people for a new friend now, and Harriet getting the new girl into trouble with her brilliant schemes. Or maybe Anna and Harriet would be each other's best friend now. I had watched them carefully the day they had come to say goodbye. They had walked away with their arms linked as if I had never been there. I still kept all our notes though, slipped in between the pages of the notebook they had given me. I could feel the edges of it in my school bag, pressing into my ankle.

'So, do you know much about World War Two survivors?' Bobby asked.

'Um, nothing really,' I muttered.

'No worries, partner. This is a job for Wikipedia,' he said, grinning.

We went to the library and there was loads of stuff about World War Two on the Internet. Bobby found lots of accounts of soldiers and Jewish families. But the best one was about the Lilliput Troupe. I liked it so much I wrote some of it down in my notebook.

The Ovitz family founded the Lilliput Troupe. The dwarf members of the family performed and the average-height members helped backstage. They travelled around entertaining people in Romania, Hungary and

Czechoslovakia. They lived by the advice their mother had given them: Through thick and thin, never separate; stick together, guard each other and live for one another. Because the Ovitz family were Jewish they were taken to concentration camps. All but one brother followed their mother's advice. He was killed, but the others survived.

There was even a stage picture of the performing dwarf family members: Avram, Freida, Micki, Elizabeth, Perla, Rozika and Franzika. The men were all in hats and shirts, and the women were in beautiful full-length dresses, holding handbags. Bobby tried to print it but the printer wasn't working, so I set about drawing them all out on to a big piece of paper for our poster. Bobby wrote 'The Lilliput Troupe' in big bubble writing across the top and started colouring in my drawings. It was nice drawing in the library. I almost forgot Mum had lost the shop and we had moved to the horrible flat with the mean girls.

By the time we had to give our presentation, me and Bobby realized we'd got a bit carried away with the drawing and hadn't done much writing. Mrs Pervis's black beady eyes seemed to be boring right through me. I knew what I wanted to say, but my mouth wouldn't make the right words. I could only mumble and Bobby just pointed to the pictures. Bobby was not very good at remembering things in front of Mrs Pervis either.

'It looks as if you two wasted your time drawing pictures. This is not art class, Sydney Goodrow. Both of you can stand on a chair with your hands on your head for the rest of the lesson.'

Bobby almost broke the chair. It made this horrifying *crack!* sound and Mrs Goodrow told him if it broke he'd have to pay for a new one, but she didn't let him get down. The rest of the class couldn't stop sniggering. My arms were starting to ache by the time Alison's group gave their presentation. It was about rations in the war. Alison reeled off a long list of things people couldn't eat.

'Ice cream . . .' she carried on in the slowest way possible.

'Oh God,' Bobby said, leaning over towards me, 'I think I would have starved back then.'

I felt a bit starved too. I hadn't eaten much before school because I had felt a bit funny. Standing on a chair wasn't helping much either. My arms were aching and my belly was rumbling and I started to feel a bit sick. Then I started to feel a lot sick. So I tried to make a dash for the loo, but Mrs Pervis jumped in front of the door.

'Where do you think you're going, Miss Good-row?'

I tried to speak and this time something came out, but it wasn't words. It was vomit and it went all over Mrs Pervis.

Ten

I got to miss school after all and so did Jade. She got kicked out on her very first day. Actually, for the record, Jade said she wasn't kicked out, she was only suspended. Mum didn't think that was much better. Although she couldn't help laughing when she found out what for. Jade had superglued the hand of the girl from the flat below to her phone. Lexi (that's her name) had been showing the picture of Jade pulling Mum up the stairs to the whole school. People started calling Jade Snow White. So in woodwork Jade put superglue all over the back of Lexi's phone when she wasn't looking. Lexi had to spend the afternoon in A & E, but people stopped calling Jade names.

Jade was suspended for the rest of the week. She'd always been a bit naughty, but she'd never been suspended before. Mum even had to go in and talk to the head teacher about the 'incident'. Lexi's mum came upstairs to yell at Jade. But Mum wouldn't let her into the flat, so she just stood in the open doorway getting madder and madder while Mum tried to reason with her. Me and Jade watched from the hallway as she turned bright red and puffed up to twice her normal size. She looked like one of those pufferfish from the Discovery Channel. I was almost convinced she was going to explode.

'You and your family move in and start causing trouble!'

Mum tried to explain. 'Mrs Patterson, from what I understand—'

'Her whole hand is bright red!'

At this, me and Jade burst into fits of laughter. Mum turned on us, wearing her 'don't mess with me' face so we ran into our bedroom. The rest of the argument was a bit of a muffle followed by the slamming of our front door. Me and Jade peeped out.

'Good start, girls,' Mum said, nodding her head sadly. 'Really good start.'

Jade opened her mouth to protest, but Mum just raised a hand and closed her eyes.

'Well, you're going to have to spend the rest of the week with Grandma, and God help you when she hears why.'

'But she totally deserved it and—' Jade started.

Mum held up her hand. 'Right. Knickers to cooking. I'm going to get fish and chips,' she said, grabbing her coat.

I was still feeling a bit sick when Mum came back with fish and chips, and Jade was being all pouty. But Mum seemed in a much better mood. She popped open the buttons of her waistcoat and breathed out a sigh of relief.

'Plates and cups, you two. I'm just going to call Grandma.'

Mum was a long time on the phone. Usually she and Grandma end up having an argument and hanging up on each other. The odd thing is, they phone each other constantly. Even if it's just to talk about what the neighbours have done. Jade said it's because secretly they like arguing with each other. It keeps them on their toes. But whatever was being said this time was mostly on Grandma's side, because all we heard from Mum was 'I'm sorry' and 'I know' and 'I'll try, Mum'.

By the time Mum got round to her chips, they were a bit on the cold side and I had only picked at mine. They were pretty good fish and chips, but it wasn't quite the same without the fortune cookies. Jade went to hunt for the bag Mr Wu had given us in some of the boxes we hadn't unpacked.

'So, apart from the whole throwing-up-at-school thing, how was your day?' Mum asked.

For some reason I didn't really want to tell her. I just shrugged and said it was OK. Mum wasn't fooled though; she put her arms around my neck and pulled me in for a proper cuddle.

'That bad, huh?'

I hate it when people cuddle me when I'm upset. It instantly makes me want to cry. I had to gulp back big fat tears.

'I think I have a bug,' I said, sniffling.

'Well, maybe you should stay home for a couple of days with Jade and Grandma. But if you're feeling better we'll go to the funfair at Clarence Pier on Saturday. You look like you need some cheering up.'

I wasn't the only one who needed cheering up.

That night I heard Mum talking to Dad. She does this when she's sad and thinks me and Jade are asleep. She sets two glasses of wine up at the kitchen table and has long conversations that sometimes go on through the night. I opened the bedroom door and watched Mum up at the kitchen table. She traced the rim of her glass and stared into space. It was taking longer than usual for her to get started tonight.

After breathing out a long breath she said, 'I lost our shop, Paul.' She sipped her wine before going on.

'I had to bring the girls to Portsmouth, but it's good to be near Mum. I know you two never really got on, but it is good for the kids to be near family. Well, I say that now . . .'

Through the crack of our bedroom door I watched as she stared at Dad's glass and her smile melted away.

'Jade's already getting into trouble, and Sydney – well, I worry about her. She's a lot like you, lives in her head too much.' She sighed heavily. 'Maybe this change will do us good?' she said, but it was a question and we both waited for an answer.

Eleven

Mum and Jade had a huge row about going to the funfair on Saturday. Mum said Jade couldn't expect to be taken out after she'd been suspended, and Jade said Grandma had spent all week yelling at her already and really it wasn't her fault she'd got thrown out. Mum went very quiet and Jade went for a sulk in the loo. Jade got her way though and instantly became all sweetness and light. She even said I could pick out something of hers to wear. Jade's clothes are so cool. She has all these amazing T-shirts with old bands on them and really tight jeans and lots of silver bracelets. It took me ages to decide. In the end Jade helped me pick out a black top with a silver thunderbolt on it and a silver heart necklace. She nodded approvingly and pushed me over to the mirror.

'Much better than those kiddie clothes – can't you see the difference?' Jade said, pretending to be the host of a makeover show. 'The black brings out your eyes and gives you a more sophisticated look.'

I looked at myself in the mirror. For once I didn't look like a Year Four and I definitely didn't look like Mum. I wasn't sure I liked it. But it was too late to change as Mum was jangling her keys eagerly.

The funfair lived up to its name. Not because it was particularly good. It was actually pretty run down and the men who worked on Clarence Pier all smelt of wet cigarettes. But I couldn't help but get excited when I saw the rides. And we did get ice cream from a proper ice-cream stall that had loads of different flavours. Mum got vanilla because she said you couldn't go wrong with a classic. Jade got a rum and raisin. Yuk! And I got a two-scoop cone: mint chocolate chip and raspberry ripple. Then we went on the rides. We each got to pick one. I picked the waltzer, which is like these super-fast spinning cups. Jade grabbed my hand and rushed me on to them before I could change my mind. I nearly threw up again.

The boy running the ride decided to push our booth so it spun extra hard. I think he did it so he could flirt with Jade. But I was screaming so hard he got fed up after a while. When we got off, me and Jade both ended up staggering sideways into the wall. Mum said she was glad she'd sat that one out. But she was annoyed when she wasn't tall enough to ride the roller coaster. She'd always been allowed on the one near our flat in London, because they were so used to us. She even tried standing on her tippy-toes, but the guy at the entrance wasn't having any of it. I didn't really fancy going on it, so I lingered behind with Mum while Jade jumped into a cart. Good thing too, because it got stuck halfway up. The man running the ride just stared at it for a bit, sniffed and went back to reading his newspaper. It took ages for it to get fixed. So me and Mum snuck off for some extra-vinegary chips in a cone.

Before we left, all three of us had a quick go on the bumper cars. We ended up being bumper champions, even though there was a sign saying no bumping. Honestly, what is the point of bumper cars without bumping? Me and Jade ended up ganging up on Mum to try to bump her. Mum was a surprisingly good driver in a bumper car though – we hardly touched her. If only she was as good a driver in the truck.

It was an almost perfect day. Almost, because of what happened in the arcades, which we had saved for last. The arcades were the proper old-fashioned type where they have penny falls. We watched a woman with a toddler jam two-pence pieces in and just miss out on winning a twenty-pound note. Mum went over to the cashier and asked for a two-pound coin to be changed into loads of 2p's. The cashier looked like she wanted to say something very rude, but she didn't – she gave Mum what she asked for. Mum gets away with a lot of things other people wouldn't. She poured us a handful of coins each and we took turns trying to win. Jade aimed for winning the notes, but I had my eye on a pink Casio watch. Jade eventually gave up and drifted off to play pinball. But with the help of Mum giving the glass top a sly thump, the watch finally tipped over. The cashier woman was not pleased.

'Hey, you're not meant to win that!' she shouted at us. 'That's glued down, that is.'

'Well, that's cheating then, isn't it?' I yelled, and me and Mum dashed off to play the zombie-killer game. Jade wandered over to us just as a large group of boys walked in. They all had high-top trainers and football-team hoodies with Jade's school crest emblazoned on the front. Jade went all funny when she saw them. She looked at me and Mum, and then she bolted out of the arcade.

One of the lads spotted her and yelled after her, 'Oi, new girl! New girl, why so shy?'

But Jade was too far away. Me and Mum rushed after her. We were pretty breathless when we caught up with her.

'What was that all about?' Mum asked.

Jade looked awkward and shrugged. So Mum smiled and tried to shrug it off too. But Jade walked far ahead of us all the way back to the truck. I tried to join her a couple of times, but she didn't seem to want me near her.

Jade and Mum had one of their silent arguments on the way home. They'd got so good at arguing that they could do it in code. Mum gave Jade a long, hard stare every time we hit a red light, while Jade pretended to be looking out of the window.

When we got into our building, Jade and Mum still weren't speaking. I closed my eyes in the hallway and took deep breaths. With every breath I imagined shrinking a millimetre. I was down ten millimetres when someone tapped me on the shoulder. I opened my eyes to see a man in a paint-splattered shirt.

'You all right there?' he said, smiling.

I could see he was holding a bunch of envelopes.

'You just moved to the top flat, right?' he said.

I nodded and he wiped a dirty hand on his T-shirt before offering it to me to shake.

'I'm Ed. I live just there,' he said, tilting his head to a door behind him.

Ed had the kind of face that looks like a waxed bowling ball. It was smooth and almost perfectly round and a little part of me wanted to touch it.

'Sydney, what are you doing?' Mum called from over the banister.

'Oh, hi,' Ed said, as Mum appeared at the bottom of the stairs again.

'You must be Amy Goodrow?' he said, looking at the letters in his hands, while giving Mum a furtive glance.

'Uh-huh,' Mum said warily as Jade slammed our front door.

'I only ask, because I think Mrs Patterson has been hiding your mail.'

'What?' Mum said.

'Yeah, I saw her stuffing it down the side of the desk,' he said, pointing to the broken table in the hall where the mail got placed. I crouched down beside it and put my hand through the crack in the back and, sure enough, I managed to slide a couple of envelopes out.

'That woman.' Mum sighed. 'Thank you. I'm Amy, as you know, and this is my daughter Sydney. The noisy one up there is Jade.'

Ed nodded at me and bent down to shake Mum's hand. 'I'm Ed,' he said. 'Come find me if you ever need anything fixed. I'm sort of the unofficial handyman around here. You're always welcome for a cup of tea too. Anyway, nice to meet you both.'

He disappeared into his flat.

Mum tore up the first letter – it was a bill. The second was addressed in green handwriting that we all recognized as Miss Peters'. It contained a flyer and a note. The flyer was an advert for the annual London Interior Art Exhibition. It had a big picture of a beautifully made wooden chair on the front, and underneath it read:

'*Showcase your furniture and hit it big! This year's best design event has got even better. Display your work and be in with a chance to win £25,000 and a spread in* Better Living *magazine.*'

Scribbled on the back of this was a note in Miss Peters' green handwriting. 'Time to get you back in the game, Amy. I'll be there to see you and your amazing work on Sunday 15 June. Love, Andrea.'

That's when I knew everything was going to be OK. Mum was going to win this. Then we would be able to get the shop back. We would move back to London and everything would go back to how it was.

Wouldn't it?

Twelve

After Miss Peters' letter I felt so happy that I almost forgot about going back to school. All my fear and worries just seemed to disappear. I felt so free I half expected my feet to just lift up from the ground. It was like I had mastered Dad's *'Floating Crane'* routine. The one where you spin around really fast, focusing on getting lighter and lighter and smaller and smaller until you can just sweep yourself off your feet. You have to grab hold of something quick or you go flying. I've tried this a couple of times in the park near our new flat and have either ended up feeling pretty pukey or falling over in a heap. But the day of the letter I felt like I could do it. I felt like I was a crane bird about to take flight. I held on to that feeling for the whole rest of the weekend. I even woke up on Monday ready to face school again. And I almost managed to walk all the way to Castle Cross without feeling like my insides were filled with angry snapping turtles. That was until I saw Alison and her gang at the school gates.

'Hey, look, it's the vomit comet!' she said, pointing and laughing.

I held my head up high and tried to look fierce, like Mum had taught me. But inside I was dying.

Alison called after me. 'Hope you didn't have a big breakfast!' And as I walked into our classroom I heard shrieks of laughter.

I tried to block out all the swirly panicky-ness in my brain, by doing a shrinking mantra over and over in my head.

Make my bones small, and my muscles strong.
Make me close to the ground so I never lose my footing.
Keep me away from the heights so I never fall to the sky.
Make my bones small, and my muscles strong . . .

I was so busy doing it and trying to calm myself down, that I didn't see Bobby sit down next to me.

'Hey, there – should I have brought protective gear? Raincoat, umbrella, maybe some goggles?' he said.

I gave him my best 'I don't know what you could be talking about' look, the one Jade uses when some of Mum's wine goes 'missing', or when I yell at her for hogging the bathroom for ages. 'You know, in case you have to upchuck again?'

'I don't want to talk about it,' I said.

Then I saw Bobby's face and felt bad about being mean to him.

'Please, can we just forget it ever happened?' I said, thinking about all the other things I wished had never happened, like coming to this school and having a clearly mad teacher.

'Why? It was classic. Her face after you ran off to the loos! It's probably the best thing I have ever seen.'

'Really?' I said.

'Yeah, she was all, like, arghhh!' Bobby said, pulling a face like one of the terrified women in the old black-and-white horror movies. 'And you were all, like, blurrrggghhh!' Bobby used his hand to illustrate a shower of sick coming from his mouth. 'Have some more, miss!'

At that moment our mad teacher suddenly appeared next to our desk.

'Robert Kowalski, is there a reason we should delay class? Or perhaps you would simply like to take over?'

The first lesson was science and Bobby didn't look tempted for a second; he just shook his head.

Mrs Pervis was in an especially bad mood that day. She kept making people stand on their chairs with their hands on their heads. Even if they just sniffled.

Bobby whispered to me that it was because at this time of year she always had her mad aunt come and visit her. And she spent all day wandering off and bringing back stray cats.

'No, it's not,' whispered one of Alison's friends. Then she leaned over and added, 'It's because this is the anniversary of when Tommy Tailor tried to flush her head down the toilet. You know, the suction in those toilets is strong enough to pull your head right off if your hair gets caught. Everyone knows that's why Mrs Pervis has her hair short.'

I was pretty sure Jade would have told me if a toilet could suck your head clean off, so I just raised my eyebrows at the blonde girl and said, 'No way.'

I was about to tell her how toilet decapitation is probably impossible, when Mrs Pervis crept up from behind and put her bony hands on my shoulders.

'Sydney, since you're so intent on talking, perhaps you can tell me how long it takes for the moon to turn once around the Earth?'

'Help,' I mouthed at Bobby, but he just shrugged. So I looked around for Harriet because she always helped me with science questions, and Anna used to squeeze my hand under the desk to reassure me when I got really frustrated over something I didn't know. But of course they weren't there. So I just mumbled the first thing that I thought sounded right.

'A year.'

'A year? My, my, Miss Goodrow, everything's a little slower in your world, isn't it? I think you will find it's twenty-eight days.'

Alison and her crew giggled, while everyone else looked terrified.

I felt my eyes begin to sting and was sure I was going to burst into tears, until Bobby nudged me and silently mimed throwing up on Mrs Pervis as she moved to the front of the class.

I had to cover my mouth to try to stop myself giggling. I was shaking so hard in my seat and making little squeaky noses into my hand that I gave up trying to hide it and pretended I was having a full-on sneezing fit.

Mrs Pervis narrowed her eyes at me, but turned back to the whiteboard and continued scribbling science facts and weird symbols that I was sure nobody could actually understand. Sometimes I wonder if teachers make it up. Maybe some days they forget what to teach, so they just use the first things that pop into their heads? Or maybe they all get together and decide to have a laugh and teach us gibberish? It's not like we would know.

Grandma would know though, because it's practically a law that grandmas know everything. Well, that's what she always says. My grandma does know a lot about science and maths, so when I got home after the terrors of Mrs Pervis, Mum invited her over to help me with my homework.

Mum's better at helping me with history and art, and Jade's quite good at helping me with geography (well, she used to be), but Grandma, it turns out, is pretty much the best at science.

She has this way of making it sound interesting. Even my old teacher Mrs Mitchell couldn't do that.

'Do you know that, right now, the Earth is being hit by all kinds of things from space?' Grandma said after we had finished my Earth, Sun and Moon homework.

It made me worried to think that stuff could randomly fall out of the sky. I hated things I couldn't predict. I didn't even like going to bed if I didn't know what cereal I was going to have in the morning.

'When your grandpa was alive, we watched meteor showers from the ships he served on in the navy. Best time to see them is on a dark and moonless night far from the lights on land. It looked like a shower of stars falling from the heavens.'

'Are you telling stories about Dad?' said Mum, coming in from the kitchen and looking like a zombie-movie extra with her chin and hands splashed with red paint. 'Don't listen to her, Sydney; they're all lies.' She winked.

'Amy, what in heaven's name have you got all over you?'

'I was playing around with an idea for a new chair design—'

'Oh,' Grandma interrupted. 'How *merveilleux*.'

'Don't be like that, Mum. There's a big competition coming up, cash prize, real exposure, it could be just the thing to put us back on track, maybe enough to get the shop back.'

I wanted to scream and shout I was so happy Mum had started making things for the competition. But Grandma had other ideas.

'But you're finally free of all that. You don't have to worry about your husband's shop any more, Amy.'

'It was our shop, Mum. I wanted it just as much as he did.'

'And what about your job? Your new start?' Grandma said. Her mouth narrowed into a thin line.

'It's not that I'm ungrateful. But the tax office! You have to admit, I'm never going to make employee of the month.'

'So you would rather be practically unemployed in that shoebox of a flat in London?'

'Frankly, yes,' Mum said, pulling herself on to her tippy-toes, her hands on her hips.

'Unemployed, two children, single mother. It was never what I imagined for you.'

'It's not exactly what I planned either!'

'Amy, if your father was here, he would be so upset for you.'

Everyone fell deathly silent and Grandma's face got all pinched up. I wasn't sure why Grandma looked so upset when she was the one being so horrible. But that's the thing about families – everyone knows exactly how to make each other cry.

Grandma picked up her handbag and let herself out. I listened to her steps as they faded away and for the first time I realized how lonely she must have been without us. I thought about her looking up at a meteor shower on a dark, moonless night, all alone without us, and just for a moment I felt bad for wanting to go back to London so much.

Thirteen

After the letter from Miss Peters Mum started working non-stop. She went to the dump and salvaged all this old wood and metal and even some old swirly Victorian railings. Ed came along to help her get it all into the truck. Mum gave him a fiver and he looked a bit embarrassed.

It was Mum who was left embarrassed next time we saw Ed though. When Mum and me popped round the next week to borrow some milk for our cornflakes, Ed insisted on making us all breakfast. Mum lied and said we were in the middle of cooking our own. Even though we only had the mushy stuff at the bottom of the cornflakes packet to eat. Ed gave me a suspicious look and I couldn't help giving us away.

'We haven't had anything but cereal for three days,' I said.

Mum turned pink, but one look at Ed's croissants and jam and she even managed to persuade Jade to come down. We all swarmed around his kitchen table. It reminded me of the ones Mum used to sell, the sort with legs in the shape of lions' paws. I started talking about Mum's furniture and then the competition got mentioned. Ed asked Mum lots of questions then. They were talking for so long we were late for school. Ed even offered to help Mum with her plans for the furniture competition. Mum would never admit it, but sometimes she gets all stiff and achy after sawing things all day. So she said she would only accept his help if he let her pay him in hot dinners. It's hardly a fair trade – Mum struggles to cook anything that's not an omelette but Ed didn't know that.

Mum was also struggling to get out of all the things Grandma kept inviting her to: single-mingle nights at the local community centre, the wine and cheese festival, even the Portsmouth French Society mixer. Mum kept having to pretend to be ill so she could work on the furniture with Ed. But even though Mum got out of half the things Grandma signed her up for, she could still only spend a couple of hours in the evenings on the furniture.

Mum doesn't get back from work until 6 p.m. So Jade had to walk me home after school. More than once, Jade had her school uniform stuffed in her bag or her jacket zipped up with trainers on. I wanted to ask where she went and if I could come, maybe. But I knew it was one of those things we don't talk about. Like when she got diarrhoea and didn't make it to the bathroom in time. Or that I still had to sleep with the light on sometimes. Or that Mum still talked to Dad. So I just pretended I didn't know and Jade pretended she didn't know I knew.

After a month I had almost got used to this new routine. It wasn't so bad walking home – I got to see all the new baby bunnies hopping about the fields opposite the motorway. But there were other days that weren't so good. The day she turned up with her friends to pick me up, me and Bobby knew she'd been bunking off. She'd forgotten to put her school tie back on, and her shoes were all muddy. Her new friends, the Troutface Twins and Hairy Henry, the boys from the arcade, looked just as sus. I knew that Henry was in Jade's class. I had never actually seen his face because his shaggy hair covers it. Jade likes him because he can play bass guitar and wears a leather jacket. He put an arm around Jade's shoulders, while the Troutface Twins stopped to light cigarettes. The Troutface Twins are Henry's older brothers, Zack and Oli. They were gross. They both had tongue piercings, and every time they talked I could see a flash of metal studs. Even Jade didn't like them that much. She was the one who came up with the nickname Troutface, because they always have their mouths half open like fish to show off their piercings. Sometimes she made jokes about them to make me feel better. But she never said anything in front of them. If I didn't know better I'd think she was scared.

'Come on, Sydney, let's go,' Jade called to me from behind the school fence. 'And tell your mate to hurry up.'

'Hey, blobby Bobby!' the twins yelled at him. 'Get a move on.'

'Um, maybe I shouldn't walk back with you today, Sydney,' Bobby said, shuffling his feet.

It made me sad to see his reluctance to be with me. Bobby was the only good thing about Castle Cross school. He was the only thing I was going to miss when Mum won the competition and we moved back to London.

'Don't be simple,' I said. 'We live in the same direction.' I took hold of Bobby's hand and gave it a squeeze.

The walk back home seemed like the longest walk ever. The Troutface Twins kept coming up with rude things to say about Bobby. I kept waiting for Jade to say something. But she didn't; she just twirled her strand of pink hair and pretended everything was OK, while the twins just kept on.

'Oi, where do you buy your clothes from, pork chop? Do you have to order them special? Does your mum have to save up for them? What's your mum feed you on? How many aeroplane seats do you have to book for your arse?'

Bobby stared hard at the pavement and kept on walking, but I could tell he was crying by the way his shoulders kept shaking. This was terrible. I'd never seen Bobby cry, not ever! He was always the one who cheered *me* up. I hated the twins for doing this. I wanted to smack them and I wanted to grab Jade and shake her. But I didn't; I just gave Bobby's hand another squeeze.

'Oi, Jade, is your sister a chubby-chaser?'

'Leave off, you two.'

For a moment I was so glad she had finally said something. But I could tell from her voice that she didn't really mean it.

'What's that, Jade?' one of the twins yelled. 'Were you just trying to look out for your little sister's fat friend?'

Then the other one shouted, 'You better watch out, Jade. If that thing gets the munchies, he'll eat her.'

I couldn't wait any longer for my sister to do the right thing. I grabbed Bobby's hand and started running. I could hear Jade calling after us but we didn't look back. We just ran and ran and ran, until I didn't know where we were.

When we finally stopped, Bobby bent over, struggling to catch his breath. I suppose he'd never moved that fast in his life. I let go of his hand and left him making wheezy sounds while I looked around to see if I could spot anything familiar. We were in a park, but it was one that I'd never seen before. It was one of those parks for little kids. The swings had little holes to put your legs, and there were animal seats that rocked on springs. There weren't any little kids around though. We were all alone. I went and sat on the mini-roundabout and slowly, eventually, Bobby came and joined me. He still looked a bit red round the eyes.

'I'm sorry 'bout my sister,' I said.

Bobby sniffed. 'S'OK.'

'She never usually lets people say stuff like that,' I said. 'She always sticks up for Mum whenever—'

Bobby interrupted me. 'Is that cos your mum's little?' he asked. 'Only I saw her drop you off on your first day.'

I nodded.

'Is your dad little too?'

'He was.'

Whenever I tell people my dad's dead they usually go all weird. Some people get embarrassed and make excuses to go somewhere else. It always makes me feel worse. And if I'm with Mum then they say stupid things like, 'It must be so hard for you with the children.' As if we are some terrible burden. That or they try to be extra nice, as if they can make up for the fact my dad's not here any more.

But Bobby didn't do any of that. I could see him sit there and think about what I'd said. Then he turned towards me. 'Hey, Sydney, did you know the biggest man who ever lived has got a life-size statue built of him in Illinois? And did you know that the smallest person ever was a woman called Caroline Crachami? She only grew to fifty centimetres.' Bobby held his hand out to show how high fifty centimetres was off the ground.

'Wikipedia?' I asked.

Bobby smiled at me and wiped his face with the sleeve of his school jumper. Then he said, 'I think I know where we are, Sydney.'

It didn't take us long to find our way home. Soon we were walking along the main road, listening to the roar of the cars as they whizzed past us.

'If I had to choose between being a giant or being tiny, I'd choose tiny every time,' Bobby yelled over the noise of the traffic. 'Sometimes,' he went on, looking at his belly, 'I actually wish there was less of me.'

Right then I wished I could tell Bobby about shrinking. But I couldn't, because then it wouldn't be my and Jade's secret any more. Even though, as I thought this, I realized that Jade had so many other secrets these days that she probably wouldn't miss ours.

Fourteen

As March came to an end, I began to feel sure that I'd grown. The waistband on all my Mr Men knickers had become uncomfortably tight. *Maybe all my growing is out, rather than up*, I thought. Perhaps I was going to end up being the world's fattest short woman, and have a statue of me put up in Illinois too. Or on Clarence Pier, next to all the neon signs from the arcades and dancing doughnut statues outside the fast-food places. I got so worried about it I tried to measure myself with Mum's metal tape measure. But I ended up hitting myself in the eye and scraping the wall with the hook at the end. And then Jade walked in on me while I was wielding the tape measure like a lightsaber in one hand and clutching my wounded eye with the other.

'Sometimes I really doubt that we are related,' she said.

After a month of helping Mum, Ed started spending more and more time at the flat. He would pop around all the time for little chats and sometimes stay for dinner. And Jade began getting really weird about it. She would slam doors for no reason, buried all my stuff under her clothes and started spending most of her free time smoking with Hairy Henry and the Troutface Twins. She didn't even like smoking. I caught her practising it in the bathroom mirror and it took her three attempts at puffing on the cigarette before she could do it without coughing.

The weekend before Easter Ed popped around for one of his chats. He talked to Mum about movies – he likes the really old horror ones. He even has T-shirts with prints of the original *Frankenstein* and *Dracula* movie posters on them. He promised to take me, Mum and Jade to the theatre outside town that does a classic horror-movie night. I wasn't sure I wanted to go. Ed's all right, but watching old movies is Mum's and my special thing. We like to eat chocolate buttons under a blanket, watching the ones where everyone has long conversations while pretending to drive.

But Ed was getting so excited talking about the horror-movie night, he didn't notice that Grandma had silently let herself in.

From the living room I saw her standing in the hallway staring through at Ed and Mum in the kitchen area, her arms folded. I could tell she and Mum were in the middle of another of their cold wars. That's what me and Jade call their fights. The ones where neither of them will speak about what they're really mad about until . . . *BOOM!* Finally one of them will explode and they'll have a big blowout. Jade's got so good at predicting when this will happen that as soon as she saw Grandma loitering outside our kitchen/living room she flashed her fingers up at me and mouthed, 'Ten minutes,' grinning.

'Hey, Grandma!' Jade yelled.

'Mum, did you just let yourself in?' Mum said.

'I knocked,' Grandma replied, striding into the kitchen area. 'I guess everyone was too *distracted* to hear,' she said, glancing at Ed.

'Mum, this is Ed.'

'Mm-hmm,' Grandma said, giving him a good look up and down.

'He's a friend,' Mum said.

'Ah, this is the man helping out and cooking breakfast for my grandchildren.'

'He's a friend, Mum,' Mum said, turning red.

'So you've mentioned.' She turned to him. 'Edward, is it? Do you think you could give me and Amy a moment alone?'

'Oh, sorry, of course. I'll speak to Amy later. It was nice to meet you, Ms Goodrow. I've heard so much about you.'

Ed winked at Mum and sauntered off. I was sure Mum had been moaning to him about Grandma.

'Well, I see you're feeling better.' Grandma put her neatly manicured hands on her hips.

'Of course I'm fine. Why wouldn't I be?' Mum replied.

'I've barely seen you, and you're not returning my phone calls. I could have had a fall or died; you wouldn't have known.'

'Don't be ridiculous, Mum.'

'What's ridiculous about it? These things happen.'

'Not to you they don't.'

'I could have been lying there at the bottom of my stairs with cats licking my face.'

'Mum! Not in front of the kids.'

'I want to hear about the cats eating Grandma,' Jade piped up as she pulled her headphones off.

'Can we not be overdramatic?' said Mum. 'Sydney's already got an overactive imagination.'

'No, I haven't,' I replied. But I *was* imagining gangs of fat ginger cats prowling around Grandma's empty house hunting for their next prey. Then the cats became tigers and lions and cheetahs, all waiting by the door for Grandma's return, their long pink tongues slowly licking their lips in anticipation. I shuddered and Jade elbowed me in the ribs.

'Well, anyway,' went on Grandma, 'I made you some soup. It's got lots of carrots and celery and real chicken stock in it. You could benefit from some proper home-made food. I know you; you can neglect to look after yourself, Amy, especially with all this running around with this Edward character.'

Jade stiffened in her chair. I wasn't sure if this was at the mention of Ed's name or because she was anticipating that this was when Mum was going to blow up and declare full-on war. But Mum did not look as if she was about to commence hostilities. She had got all fidgety and started chewing her lip the same way I do when I'm nervous. Which is a lot, since I have a mad teacher, a bad sister and have left everyone I have ever known back in London.

'So how much time have you been spending with this man?' Grandma continued.

'I need a cup of tea. Does anyone else want a cup of tea? Tea?' Mum said. 'I think we should all have tea.'

Grandma kept looking at Mum and then at Jade. It made Jade start fidgeting and pulling at her strand of pink hair.

'Are the two of them *close*?' Grandma asked Jade.

Jade pushed herself up from her chair and gave Mum her death-ray look. If looks could kill, my sister would be a seriously dangerous weapon. Then she stomped off to our room and slammed the door. The whole flat rattled and Grandma stood over Mum with a very disapproving look on her face.

'Earl Grey, anyone?' Mum asked. 'Or maybe something herbal?'

'Don't take this the wrong way, Amy,' said Grandma in her most condescending voice, 'but don't you think this man is a little too . . . a little too . . . how should I put this . . .?'

'Camomile, peppermint, sleepy-time tea, we have them all . . .' Mum carried on, a weak smile on her face, like she was trying to be brave, the way you do when you fall over in front of everyone and have to get up real quick to show you're not hurt.

I held my breath, waiting for Grandma to drop the bomb.

'A little too . . . *bald* for you?' Grandma finished.

Mum and me burst out laughing, the kind of laugh that comes out at first like a little wheeze because you have been all wound up, expecting the worst.

After we had stopped laughing and Grandma had left (to feed her cats, I hoped), I started wondering what Grandma had meant about Ed, and why everyone had got so weird. Did Grandma think Ed and Mum were dating? But they were just friends, right? Mum still loved Dad. Didn't she? Everything was so confusing and I felt sure none of these things would be happening if we were back home where we belonged. If we were in London, then Miss Peters would have been able to explain things to me, because she's read all the dating-advice books in the world and understands relationships. She could have helped me to spot the signs to see if something was going on between Mum and Ed.

I tried to ask Jade when I got into bed that night, but she wouldn't talk to me. She never talked to me any more. She just said, 'It's bad enough we have to share a room, but don't think that means I have to talk or even acknowledge that you exist.'

We never do any of our sister things any more, like sitting and chatting at the window, or telling stories about Dad, or Jade dressing me up in her clothes and painting little skulls on my nails, or playing music really loud and jumping around till we feel sick.

Back in our London flat I used to sit on the end of Jade's bed and talk for ages about stupid stuff, while she did her homework or tuned her guitar. And when we fought (which I think sisters do more often than boxing kangaroos) she used to yell at me, not just ignore me. It was like she was becoming some different kind of person.

So instead of relying on Jade to tell me anything important any more, I decided I would just have to do it myself. That night I made a list in my head of signs that could show if Mum ever did actually have a boyfriend, based on what I had seen watching old movies and on one of the romance books Mr Wu had given to Mum.

- When you get romanced your bosoms heave.

Well, bosoms are boobs, and I hadn't noticed Mum's doing anything weird.

- People having a passionate affair get ravished.

I have no idea what ravished is, but I'm pretty sure Ed is not capable of it.

- People in love start dressing better, not wearing glasses and wearing their hair down.

Well, there was no sign of that one either, because Mum still used her huge 1980s reading glasses, had her hair up in a messy bun when she worked and had been wearing the same Mickey Mouse T-shirt and paint-splattered dungarees two days in a row.

But she did seem different, and Ed *was* spending a lot of time around our flat.

I wondered what Dad would have thought of this.

I wondered what Jade really felt about it too. I wondered if she was feeling as confused and swirly and odd as I was, as if someone had mixed up all my insides. Or maybe the old Jade had been completely replaced by the new Jade and she didn't really *have* feelings any more at all.

Fifteen

After Easter Jade stopped picking me up from school. She only came by to check I wouldn't tell Mum she wasn't walking me home and to make sure I covered for her. Instead of taking me home, she went off with Hairy Henry and the Troutface Twins. Apparently everyone at Jade's school is scared of the Troutface Twins and now everyone is scared of Jade too. Even the girl from downstairs. This has made Jade one of the most popular girls in school.

To be popular you have to wear a non-existent skirt, hang around with idiots and not do any schoolwork. Having boobs helps too. I couldn't imagine ever being popular, let alone having boobs.

Even though she was pretty awful and even

though she started calling me a ginger, or 'ginga' (which I'm not – my hair is reddish brown), Jade was still my sister. Without her I felt like there was a bit of me missing. Though maybe only a small bit, like a thumb or a toe. I wished I could talk to Mum about it, but she was so busy with work and the furniture competition there was never any time for me.

Sometimes I felt all alone. So I tried to think about Dad and what he would say. He would probably tell me that families stick together, no matter what. But I didn't think Jade wanted to be a part of our family any more. Then I remembered about the Ovitz family, the famous dwarf performers who all survived the Holocaust. Well, all but one.

At the end of April, when all the trees outside my school were in blossom, I watched Jade go off with Hairy Henry. He had his arm draped heavily across her shoulder, and the Troutface Twins followed like their shadows. I got this sick, panicky feeling. It was the same feeling I got when I thought about what Grandma said about things falling to Earth from space.

I'd mentioned this to Bobby as we walked away from school, and he'd said, 'You know only one person was ever hit by a meteor from space.'

The cars roared past us, and in the distance I heard Jade laughing along with one of the twins.

'Ann Elizabeth Hodges from Alabama – came right through her roof. She was fine though; she didn't get squished or anything. They named the meteorite after her and she's on Wikipedia and everything too. Some people are so lucky.'

But I didn't think Ann Elizabeth Hodges was lucky. I just thought about how she had probably got up in the morning thinking it would be another normal day. How she was probably making a cup of tea, or taking a nap, or thinking about what shopping she needed to do and then *BOOM!* A meteor hits her.

Suddenly the cars sounded very loud and everything started to spin. The iron school gates, the empty playing field, the road and even Bobby. It was like the moment after you dive from the top of a roller coaster. My heart felt like it was in my throat, my hands felt all shaky and sweaty.

I closed my eyes and tried to do the '*Falling*

Horse'. I breathed a deep breath in and then let it out as slowly as possible while folding myself into the smallest shape I could get into. I wrapped my arms around my stomach and folded my legs underneath me, until I was crouching on the pavement. The cold seeped up from the street.

'Hey, you all right?' I heard Bobby say. 'You look like you're going to be sick again.'

I balled my hands into fists and shook my head. Bobby sat down next to me and waited. That's the good thing about Bobby; he doesn't make you talk when you don't want to. If it was Harriet or Anna they would demand to know what was wrong and I wouldn't know what to tell them. I didn't really know myself. I just felt like I was waiting for the next bad thing to happen. For something to come flying out of the sky and hit us.

Once our bums were completely numb from sitting on the cold pavement, Bobby said, 'You wanna go down the seafront? It always makes me feel better.'

'My mum gets back in an hour,' I replied.

'Ah, that's loads of time. We can even get chips. Come on.'

He got up first and pulled me up. Then we trudged up to the bus stop at the top of the road. The number 23 soon came and we clambered on and sat at the back, watching our neighbourhood go by as we travelled closer to the sea.

I had seen the sea with Mum and Jade when we'd gone down to the funfair and the pier. But I had never sat on the beach before. Even though it was starting to rain a bit, and my chips were getting a bit soggy, it was wonderful.

I guess you forget how big the sea is if you don't see it. It was blue rippling waves going far off until they hit the sky. And all the boats and ships and little islands looked so small and far away. It reminded me of the story Dad had told me and Jade called 'The Faraway Land'.

On the edge of the world is an almost mythical place called the Faraway Land. On a clear day, standing on top of the highest mountain, looking directly north, you can just about see it. Glimmering palaces and towers lit by tiny stars, just behind a cloud of mist. Long ago, it's said, two men set off in search of the Faraway Land.

Manik was a warrior. At seven foot tall, with arm muscles the size of most men's heads, it was claimed he had been chiselled out of the side of a mountain by the gods themselves. The other man was Talock. He was old and wizened and in size barely reached Manik's knee. Nobody expected him to make it to the Faraway Land, if it did indeed exist. While Manik mounted his huge black horse and rode north to the cheers of his home town, Talock had quietly set off by boat.

Ten years later, Manik still was riding north. He felt no closer to the Faraway Land than the day he had set off. So he decided to stay at the next little village he stopped at. It was there that he got married, bought a farm and built a house for his wife and baby son. It was another five years before he even thought about the Faraway Land, the place you can see sometimes just out of the corner of your eye, when he saw Talock again.

Talock was barely recognizable when Manik bumped into him in as he was passing through the village. Wanting to show the old man how well he had done, Manik invited him into his home. It seemed to Manik that Talock was even smaller and more wizened than he remembered from all those years ago. But Talock's bright eyes were unmistakable. Manik had thought that it was incredible he was even still alive, but what Talock brought out of his pockets shocked the big man even more. For there, placed *on his kitchen table, were tiny glittering stars taken from the spires and roofs of the Faraway Land's towers.*

'But how did you make it there?' Manik had demanded.

And Talock had replied, 'When you're this small and this slow, everything's far away. So you know to just keep going.'

I can remember Dad telling me this story, even though my memories of him are becoming a bit blurry now. But I can still clearly picture his hands, the way they darted about. Dad always told stories with his hands.

I was still thinking about this, looking out across the sea, when Bobby squeezed my shoulder. 'Sydney, we've got to run if we're going to make the bus back home in time.'

He grabbed my hand, and as we raced breathlessly over the beach, I knew I would be late.

When I did get home Mum was standing by the door, her raincoat half on, half off. I could tell by the look on her face that she was furious.

'Where the hell have you been? Jade said she couldn't find you after school. I've been worried sick. I was just about to send out the search dogs.'

I looked at Jade, who stared at her feet as if her

Converse were the most exciting and riveting thing she had ever seen. I opened my mouth to tell Mum about how Jade had left me to go off with Henry, or to tell her about seeing the sea and how small it had made me feel, or to tell her about how much I missed her, but none of those words wanted to come out. All I could manage was, 'I got a bit lost.' Truth was, I did feel a bit lost. I must have looked it too, because instead of yelling at me some more Mum looked as if she was going to cry.

'Oh, Sydney, I shouldn't be mad at you. It's my fault. No more working late. From now on I'm going to be with my girls.'

'But the furniture . . .' I almost yelled, as panic bubbled up.

'Can be done at the weekend; you two can even help. Wouldn't hurt Jade to see a little less of her new friends and a little more of us anyway.'

Jade scowled and elbowed me in the ribs. On the way to our room she hissed in my ear, 'You ruin everything. I wish you had never been born.' Then she slammed the door in my face.

'Does that girl have to be so dramatic? Gets that from her grandma, I s'pose,' Mum said, shaking her head. 'How about you and me watch a really bad old movie?'

And even though I desperately wanted to, I just shrugged.

'We can break out the emergency chocolate,' she said, and I watched her reach to the back of the kitchen cupboard and pull out an enormous bag of milky buttons.

But I still just shrugged. I didn't feel like pretending everything was OK.

'Come on, Sydney, give me a break here. I know you and your sister have been having a hard time of it, but I'm trying my best.' Mum swaddled me in a bear hug. 'I could use a little help,' she whispered in my ear, 'and a lot of chocolate.'

But even after I got under the big old afghan blanket, knowing we were going to eat all of the chocolate buttons and practise our 1960s movie-star voices along with the film, all I could think about was that when Mum cuddled me, her arms didn't reach all the way around any more.

Sixteen

I had that dream again, the one where I keep growing and growing till my head touches the sky. Everyone I know is watching as I get further and further away from the ground. I keep calling out to Mum and Jade but they just smile and wave. Then I see Dad, and he tries to yell something but I'm too far away to hear him. I just keep travelling up and up and the clouds keep getting closer. I try to yell back down to him, but I can't see him any more.

That's when I woke up and realized I was still yelling, 'Dad!' My heart was *thud-thud-thudding* and I was all prickly with sweat.

'Jade,' I called out. But there was no answer.

'Jade, are you awake?' I asked, but there was no reply.

I sat up and peered into the darkness.

I flicked the light switch on and there was no Jade-shaped lump in her bed. The covers were all thrown back and her guitar was gone.

I got up and tiptoed out to the living room, but the lights were all switched off and there was no sign of Jade. The kitchen was empty too, apart from two wine glasses left out on the table. One of them was still full.

When I checked the bathroom I found she wasn't there either. So I sat on the toilet and tried to understand what was going on.

I did my best to think about where Jade might be. When that didn't help, I tried to think of what she might be doing. But I realized the truth was I didn't know Jade very well any more and neither did Mum.

After she had yelled at Jade the other day for messing about with Ed's tools, I heard her say under her breath, 'The older you get, the less I know you.' But I'm pretty sure what Mum had meant by 'older' was *taller*.

I stared down at my stretched-out moon pyjamas. There was an island of skin gaping between my pyjama top and bottoms. I couldn't believe how much I had grown. The more I thought about it, the louder my heart beat. I closed my eyes and tried to do a shrinking exercise, but all I could sense was my body growing. I punched my fists against the wall to try to make myself concentrate, and then something hit me on the head. It was a white pot covered in dust.

I turned it over in my hands. The label said 'Minimizer Cream'. I knew that 'minimize' meant shrink. The rest of the label read: 'To minimize blemishes and tighten areas of skin.' I looked at the area of white belly showing between my pyjama top and bottoms. *It can't hurt to try*, I thought. So I scooped some out and rubbed it into my face. There was still plenty left on my hands, so I took my top off and rubbed great creamy circles on my belly. Then I wriggled out of my pyjama bottoms and dolloped some on both my legs.

While I was bent over rubbing goop into my knees, the bathroom door swung open and there stood Jade, a large orange key ring hanging out of her pocket.

'What the hell?!' she cried.

I stood up straight, the cream going cold on my skin. 'Where have you been?' I asked.

'Why are you naked?'

I grabbed the nearest thing to cover myself, but it turned out to be a flannel.

'You are a weird child,' Jade said. Then she noticed the upturned tub of cream.

'Mum is going to kill you,' she said.

'Mum is going to kill *you*,' I replied, 'when I tell her you've been out all night.'

Jade stood in the bathroom doorway and started playing with the orange key ring.

'I'm not the only one who's been getting into Mum's stuff,' I said. 'That's the key to the lock-up.'

Jade breathed out heavily and I could smell cigarettes and cider. She smelt like the old men down at the pier.

'Help me with my pyjamas,' I said.

'She's not going to find out,' Jade said, rolling the key in her hand.

'I have to tell her.'

'You're not going to say a thing,' Jade replied. 'You know why? Because you just used up the last present Dad ever gave to Mum. He gave her that expensive anti-ageing cream as a joke on her thirty-fifth birthday. He said she was still as pretty as the day he met her. That loving him kept her young. Mum's never been able to throw it out.'

'You're lying!' I shouted.

'I wouldn't lie about Dad,' Jade said.

Grandma had tried to make Mum throw out most of Dad's stuff. But Mum had hidden things, like a box of Dad's drawings, or his blue cable-knit sweater that she still slept with under her pillow. If she had kept this it must have been important to her. I tried to scoop the cream back into its pot. But it was too late – it was almost all gone.

Jade shook her head, turned and disappeared into the dark hallway.

All I could think to do was hide the pot on the top shelf of the bathroom cupboard where Mum couldn't reach.

But when I got back into bed I started to feel really guilty. Every time I thought of Mum, it was like a tornado in my stomach. I couldn't get to sleep until I'd decided to tell her everything in the morning.

But when I was getting dressed the next morning, I noticed something wonderful had happened. When I put on my school shirt it came down to my knees. I must have shrunk during the night. The cream had worked!

Nobody else seemed to notice. Over the breakfast table, Mum rushed around making us omelettes while Jade was busy staring daggers at me.

'Don't say a word,' she mouthed. But I was so happy I didn't care.

Seventeen

Just before summer half-term, and with only three weeks to go, Mum and Ed finally finished the furniture showpieces. Our living room was filled with the most amazing things. Ed and Mum had created from scratch a huge iron bed with big crystal baubles on the bedposts. Next to that was a green-leather swivel armchair that looked like something from Doctor Who's Tardis. But best of all was a fancy little couch.

'Behold *une chaise longue*,' Ed said in a very bad French accent.

'It's in between a couch and a bed. Only not as comfortable as either,' Mum said, laughing.

The chaise longue was covered in yellow buttery leather, with a slopey back and a big padded arm you could rest your head on. It looked like something you might lie on in an old-fashioned doctor's office. To finish off it had curved wooden feet that shone like polished conkers. Next to it was a matching yellow footstool. It was very posh.

'And this, Sydney,' Mum said, opening a hidden drawer in the footstool, 'is where you can keep all your secrets.'

'It would take a bigger drawer than that,' I mumbled.

But Mum didn't hear me because she was bent over the footstool, taking something out of the drawer. When she straightened up, I could see she was holding a cardboard box. From this she produced Mr Wu's fortune cookies. 'I know I've been busy lately,' she said, 'but now it is done – now that it's all finished – I can focus on my girls.'

Then, grinning like a mad thing, she tossed a fortune cookie at each of us.

Jade didn't even try to catch her cookie. She just prodded the chaise longue and said, 'It's different to the stuff you used to make.'

'I know,' said Mum, 'but I thought it was time for a change.'

'I thought you hated making average-sized furniture,' Jade said.

'Well, maybe your mum doesn't mind average size so much any more,' Ed said, putting a hand gently on Mum's shoulder. Mum turned red and Jade made a sick sound. We all heard it, but Jade saved anyone from having to say anything by storming off to our bedroom. After we heard the door slam, we could hear her strumming on the guitar and singing a really rude song about Ed.

Mum looked at Ed and shrugged. 'It's just a phase,' she said. 'She'll outgrow it soon enough.'

But, I thought to myself, Mum didn't understand the problem. Jade had grown *into* this.

'Maybe she'll come out when she hears us celebrating,' Ed said, putting an old rock CD on to drown out Jade's row. It was Deep Zeppelin or Led Purple or something. Ed played it all the time. I kind of liked it. Ed came over to me and swept me on to his feet. He likes to dance with someone standing on his feet. It was fun rocking to his old music. Mum started dancing with us and pretty soon I had forgotten about Jade's latest scene.

After a couple of songs Ed insisted on going out

for food. But even by the time he came back with fish and chips Jade still had not come out of her room. So we ate without her, the three of us snuggled up under the afghan blanket, watching an old movie on TV. It was Mum's favourite type. The kind where everyone smokes too much and women cry in the rain. The kind Jade hates. In this one the leading lady had a sofa made out of a bathtub. Ed and Mum got really excited about this. Mum asked me what I thought about having one of those in our living room. I said it didn't look very comfortable.

At the end of the film, Mum cried when the leading lady and man kissed. When I reached for the tissues for her, I saw Ed holding her hand.

Then Mum jumped up and decided she had to urgently go and do the washing-up. Which was strange, because she usually leaves it for the morning when it's just a takeaway. To be honest, sometimes she leaves it for days. If it was up to me we'd just throw the plates away and buy new ones.

Ed followed Mum out to the kitchen. I could hear him offering to help, but she sounded all flustered. He came back into the room looking confused. Then we heard a crash. And when we both ran into the kitchen Mum had slipped off the chair that she'd been standing on and had fallen against the sink. She was on the floor rubbing a very bruised lip.

Ed and I pulled her to her feet.

'Oh, damn this kitchen!' she cried. 'And this flat and this bloody world. Everything in it is just too big.'

I couldn't tell from her voice if she was going to cry or laugh. And then I saw her lip wobble and I knew she was going to cry. But Mum never cries in front of anyone, and Ed was right there. I wanted to just stop everything and make it all right, but I couldn't. And suddenly I felt like crying too. Ed put his hand gently on my shoulder.

'Looks as if your mum's been fighting the kitchen cupboards again.'

Mum gave her smallest, weakest smile.

'Ouch, you are going to have a boxer's lip,' Ed said, bending down and tilting Mum's chin to examine her face.

Mum snorted and wiped her nose on her sleeve. 'What will the neighbours say?'

'Let's get something on it before you're the talk of the street.'

I helped him wrap some ice in a tea towel, and he held it to Mum's poor swollen lip. For once she didn't complain that she was being fussed over. She even let Ed brush her hair away from her face. 'I'm going up to London tomorrow to see that band I told you about,' he said, 'but when I get back, you and me will go about making this place more little-person-friendly. What do you say?'

Mum gave a shy smile and nodded. Then Ed said, 'Well, it's getting late now, so I will have to love you and leave you, ladies. Goodnight, and thanks for a lovely evening.'

Then he picked Mum up from the kitchen chair and gave her a hug. He's the only person who Mum lets do this. Everyone else has to bend down to hug her. Grandma always complains it will be the death of her back.

Mum straightened her top and we listened to Ed's footsteps fade.

It was hard getting into bed that night because even our room had become Mum's workshop. Ed's tools were still scattered everywhere. Jade had shoved most of them on to my bed. I could tell she was pretending to be asleep. I didn't want to talk to her. Before I got into bed I left the door open so she wouldn't wake me up when she snuck out.

It wasn't Jade that woke me up, it was Mum. She was talking to Dad again, with the living-area door open. I pushed our bedroom door wide and got back into bed to listen. In the light from the hallway I could see Jade sit up too.

'The girls are getting so big. You wouldn't know them any more.' My stomach did a flip at this. I knew how disappointed Dad would be in me.

'Jade is at that difficult age. Always testing me. Testing everyone, I think.'

Jade made a snorting noise and I glared at her to be quiet.

'Sydney — she's more and more like you every day.'

Mum went silent for a long time and we waited.

Then we heard her say, 'I feel things have to move on.'

We held our breath so we wouldn't miss a word.

'Maybe it's not being in our shop. Maybe it's starting out on my own again.'

We could a high ringing sound. It was Mum running a wet finger around the rim of her wine glass. A trick Dad had taught her. It was almost like she was trying to make him answer her.

Mum sighed. 'I think this might be the last time I'm going to talk to you like this.'

I thought my heart had literally stopped beating.

'I think it's time,' she said, 'to say goodbye.'

In shock I listened to Mum get up and the squeak of her pushing back the kitchen chair, and I rushed to shut our bedroom door. In the darkness of our room, I heard Jade throw herself from her bed. When she moved to the window, her eyes glinted in the moonlight. Then she exploded. It was like watching a Coke bottle that had been shaken. She whipped around, grabbed one of Ed's tools and threw it out of the open window.

Below, we heard a crunch. The spanner had smashed Mum's truck window.

'Do you know what you've done?' I whispered angrily.

Jade slumped back into bed without saying a

word. We both knew I wouldn't tell on her and we both knew why. I got back under the covers feeling hot and angry. I hated my sister. Hated her!

I tried to do a shrinking exercise. I tried to focus on curling and uncurling my fingers and toes. But I ended up curling and uncurling my hands into tight sweaty fists. I knew why it wouldn't work. I wanted to hit Jade. I wanted to hit her really hard in her big fat sulky face.

I listened to the crumple as she pulled the covers over her head. She was making sniffling noises. Then she was making gulping ones and that's when I realized – Jade was crying.

Eighteen

Things only got worse. At breakfast no one mentioned Mum's night-time conversation. But Jade glared at Mum and spooned such big mouthfuls of cornflakes into her mouth that milk dribbled out of the corners.

'Jade!' Mum snapped. 'Do you have to eat like that?'

'I don't know,' replied Jade. 'Do I?'

'Fine, eat your cornflakes like a cow. But you're going to ruin your uniform.'

'Maybe I want to. Maybe I want to do what the hell I like. You do!'

She stormed off to the bedroom. When she returned she was wearing one of my school skirts. I stared at her with my mouth open. My skirt comes down to my knees, but on Jade it just about covered her lady bits. That is until she bent over in front of Mum and made a rude noise. Then we could both see she was wearing Mr Men knickers.

Mum laughed and said, 'You're not wearing that outside. Now go back and take off your sister's school skirt, Jade. You'll stretch it.'

'No,' hissed Jade. 'We're doing what we want, remember?'

Mum hopped down from her chair and started to chase Jade around the kitchen, grabbing at her waist and trying to force the skirt off. I tried to focus on my morning shrinking routine. But then Mum pulled Jade on to the floor and the two of them started rolling under the kitchen table. Jade was screaming blue murder and my bowl of cereal was getting rocked all over the place.

I went and locked myself in the bathroom. I climbed into the bathtub and tried not to listen to Mum and Jade screeching at each other.

'Don't think you're too big for me to smack you!' I heard Mum yell.

I stood on the side of the bath and I reached for

the tub of shrinking cream from its hiding place. I knew there wasn't much left, so after I stripped off, I carefully rubbed the last of it in. I managed to cover my body in a thin layer, all apart from my bum. There wasn't enough for my bum. I wondered if only my bum would grow. If I'd stay small but my bum would keep getting bigger and bigger. It would keep growing until I became the enormous bum lady. I'd always be falling over backward, and people would move away from me on the bus.

There was a *bang* from outside the bathroom. I wrapped a towel around myself and slowly opened the door. Jade was now standing on the kitchen table. She still had my skirt on. Mum stood in the middle of the kitchen panting. Two knocked-over chairs lay on either side of her.

'Right, Jade,' she said, 'if we are all now doing what we want, I feel like changing my hair.'

She rooted around in one of the boxes of stuff in the kitchen that hadn't yet been unpacked and came up holding Jade's pink hairspray. She popped the cap off and held the can to her head.

'You wouldn't dare,' Jade said, her eyes wide.

'If you can look ridiculous, Jade, then so can I,' shouted Mum.

The can hissed into life. When the cloud of spray settled, Mum's head was completely pink. Even her ears.

'Right,' she said, 'I'm ready now. Let's get you two off to school. Sydney, put your uniform back on – that towel is not warm enough even in this weather.'

I threw on my clothes, and Jade and me followed Mum outside. In all the fuss, I had forgotten about the truck. Its windscreen was completely caved in. Little bits of glass glinted off the front seats.

'Oh hell's bells!' shouted Mum. 'I bet it's that foul woman from downstairs. I'll have to take it to the garage after work.'

I watched Jade but she said nothing. She just nibbled at her hair.

'Well, there's nothing for it,' said Mum. 'We can hardly use the truck with all that broken glass everywhere. I'll have to walk you to school. Couldn't have picked a better day for it, Jade.'

'I don't need you to walk me,' said Jade. 'I can take myself. You look after the baby.'

She started strutting off, but Mum grabbed her arm in a fierce lock and the three of us marched together side by side.

'It's good to be out in the fresh air,' said Mum, tossing her still damp pink hair. 'Gives us a chance to catch up on things. Do you know, Jade, I got a very funny phone call yesterday from one of your teachers?'

Jade looked straight ahead and tried to pull away, but Mum clung on like a limpet.

'Apparently,' Mum said, 'you've been sick rather a lot lately. It's meant you've missed rather a lot of school. So to make sure that you don't come down with anything nasty on the way to school, Jade, I'm going to march you right to the school gate.'

We all walked on in silence. Jade and Mum were more jogging than walking. It puffed me out to keep up. When we got close to Jade's school, I was very aware of all the people looking at us. Mum's hair was all gummed together in pink spikes, and pink dye was dripping off her ears and down her neck. A group of girls stopped in the middle of the road and started laughing. A boy on his bike couldn't stop staring and rode into a lamp post.

Mum would not let go of Jade's arm, even when we got to the school entrance. I could see the teachers on the gate turn to whisper to one another. But Mum kept marching on into the playground. Jade pulled the hood on her coat tight around her face, and I felt my face burning to the roots of my hair.

That's when the Troutface Twins and Hairy Henry spotted us. Hairy Henry's jaw dropped, making him look even more like a caveman than usual.

The Troutface Twins nudged each other. 'Oh, look – Jade's brought the circus to town,' they shouted. 'Roll up, roll up.'

'Quit it, you guys,' Hairy Henry yelled. But they ignored him and started humming a circus tune really loudly.

Some of the other kids started joining in. It got louder as we got closer to the school doors. Out of the corner of my eye I saw Hairy Henry shrug at Jade.

At the top of the steps Jade hissed at Mum. 'Why did you have to let them see you?'

Mum dropped her arm as if she had been slapped in the face.

'Why can't you be normal?' Jade said. 'Why do you have to be such a freak?'

Mum made a funny gurgling noise. I could tell she was trying to say something, but Jade spun away and ran inside.

Mum turned us around and we walked back down the school steps. Most of the kids had shut up, and the teachers were bustling about by now. I could see one of them talking to the Troutface Twins. Walking to the gates took forever. Mum kept hold of my hand all the way. And she kept hold as we walked on to my school. I hadn't let her do that for ages. It reminded me of when her and Dad used to hold my hands and swing me as we walked along. I squeezed Mum's hand back and hoped no one from my school spotted us. Especially Alison and her gang.

'I'll just drop you here so your friends don't see me,' Mum said, reading my mind.

I wanted to tell her that I didn't mind that she was little. In fact, I thought it was fantastic. That I was working on it myself. So she shouldn't worry because I'd never turn into Jade. But I saw Alison's mum's car coming round the corner, so I didn't. I just nodded my head and Mum left.

Mum was in when we got home. The furniture had been taken to the lock-up, so she was sitting on the blanket in the middle of our empty living room. She was holding the spanner Jade had thrown from the window. She held it up and Jade flushed bright red.

'You're grounded, Jade,' she said. 'Forget going out and seeing your friends. Forget going to the shops. You're going to spend half-term here, in your room, doing homework.'

'You can't do that!' Jade screeched, flinging her bag on the floor.

Mum didn't even blink.

'Your father would be so disappointed in you.'

'What do you care about Dad?' Jade cried.

I closed my eyes and sucked in a breath. As I breathed out, I felt myself getting smaller. I imagined becoming so small I wouldn't be able to understand what they were saying. Their words would just be this loud background noise. Like the roar of the wind, or the sound of waves crashing against the shore.

But I could still hear the sharp words ringing in my head as I went to bed, and that night I dreamed of Dad again. But he didn't look how I remembered him. He wasn't pale or skinny, he was bright and bouncy. He was wearing the blue cable-knit jumper Grandma had made him. He was looking out of our window. He turned and tried to say something to me. But I couldn't make it out, because there were lots of people in the background all speaking at the same time. Dad kept mouthing the same thing over and over at me. I squinted and tried to follow the shapes his lips were making. My head ached. I wished the people behind would be quiet. And it was as if they heard my thoughts, because everything went silent and suddenly Dad's voice broke through. 'Get up,' he yelled. 'Get up!'

I jumped up in my bed, half expecting Dad to be standing by the window. But the room was empty. Jade was gone again. Secretly I hoped she wouldn't come back. The curtains waved in the breeze, casting shadows across my bed. I shook myself awake and stood up to shut the window. My heart was hammering and I was shaking from head to toe. I leaned against the window frame to steady myself and stared out into the night sky. But tonight it wasn't lit by street lamps or stars; it was lit by fire. A yellow haze was spreading across the hill. And as I squinted harder I could see the smoke gathering into great long plumes, and it was coming from the little orange lock-ups. The lock-ups were on fire!

Nineteen

'Muuummm!!!' I screamed, flinging her bedroom door open.

'Get up! Get up now!'

She turned over and mumbled something, still half asleep.

'Jade's in danger,' I yelled, shaking her.

Mum's eyes came to life and she sat up and grabbed my shoulders. 'Explain,' she said.

'I should have told you before, but I didn't because I couldn't and now it's all my fault. And Jade will probably get burned alive and—'

'Sydney, focus,' Mum said, giving me a shake. 'What's wrong with Jade?'

I took a deep breath and tried to get my thoughts un-muddled. 'She's snuck off to the lock-up with her friends and it's on fire,' I said.

Mum looked at me blankly for a moment, before launching herself up and out of the bed and then towards the front door, grabbing her sweatshirt from a chair on the way.

'Call the fire brigade,' she yelled, dashing down the stairs. I grabbed her mobile and rushed after her, slipping down the stairs and stumbling out on to the cold pavement.

When I dialled 999, the wait for them to answer felt like at least an hour. Then a woman's voice on the other end asked what service I wanted, and all I could think of for an answer was, 'There's a fire.'

The operator sounded quite surprised and worried that there was a real fire, or maybe she just didn't believe me. So it took ages to explain where it was. And all the time I could see Mum banging on the dashboard of the car the garage had sent round as a replacement for our truck, trying to get it to go.

'Damn it!' she cried. 'This car, this stupid car they've left me. It doesn't have any extension pedals!'

I got off the phone to emergency services and ran to join Mum. The wind whipped against my nightgown. Mum got out of the useless car and put an arm around my waist and we just stood there holding each other, and I felt so guilty about what I'd wished for earlier, that Jade wouldn't come back.

I squeezed my eyes shut and balled my hands into tight little fists. But this time I didn't think shrinking thoughts; I thought of a plan. When I opened my eyes I knew what I had to do.

I jumped into the driver's seat and then slipped down into the space under the seat. Bent forward and put my feet on the pedals.

'Mum, I can sit under the seat and work the pedals, and you can steer.'

There was no time to argue. Mum nodded and wriggled over me and swung her legs either side of my head.

'Right, you do exactly what I tell you, Sydney. Remember: right pedal go, left pedal stop.'

I pressed down on the right pedal with my foot and the car bunny-hopped forward, then stalled.

'Hang on,' Mum yelled, and she slid over and wrestled with the handbrake. 'It'll go faster if I take the handbrake off!' Then she said more quietly, 'Thank God there's no traffic at this time of night.'

I eased my feet up and down on the pedals to Mum's commands and we shot through the night.

'Left pedal! Left pedal! Brake!' Mum screamed as we careened through the gates to the lock-ups. I stamped both feet on the left pedal and the car skidded to a halt, leaving long black tyre marks behind us. Smoke billowed from the neighbouring lock-ups. Behind the cloud of smoke I could just make out two figures. They lurched towards the car like the walking dead, coughing and spluttering. It was the Troutface Twins. Mum threw open the driver's door and snapped at them, 'Where's Jade?'

'I thought she and Henry were right behind us,' one of them replied.

'She must have gone back to put out the fire,' the other twin said.

'She's still in there?' I cried, looking at the orange flames licking the rooftops.

'So's Henry!' both the twins shouted together. 'He must have gone back to help Jade.'

'All of you, get in the car!' Mum ordered, waving her arms at the twins. 'And stay in there till I get back.'

And this time the twins didn't pull faces or make fun of Mum, they just did as she said. I was the one who wouldn't listen to her.

'But, Mum, I have to help.'

'That's my job, Sydney. Now get in the car.' Then she pushed me into the back seat with the twins and locked the doors. I tried to get the door open, but it wouldn't budge; the child lock was on. I pressed the button for the window but it wouldn't work either. All I could do was watch. Mum dunked her sweatshirt into a bucket of rainwater someone had left by the lock-ups and tipped it over her head before heading into the smoke. I watched and waited.

The Troutface Twins kept trying to apologize. 'I thought I'd put my fag out. I swear it was out.'

But I wasn't listening. I pressed my face to the window and watched. My breath made little half-moon-shaped marks on the glass. I made a deal with myself that by the time the mark faded Mum and Jade would be back. I held my breath and

157

waited. The moon mark faded. One of the Trout-face Twins started to cry.

The smoke was getting thicker; it swirled all around the car and the smell of it came in through the closed windows. I could hear a siren. But it still sounded far away.

'They're not going to make it in time, are they?' the twin next to me said.

'My mum's coming back with Jade and Henry. She's coming back with them,' I shouted, grabbing his cold hand.

But Mum didn't appear and I felt like crying too.

'She's been ages,' the other twin said, biting his lip.

But I didn't know how long it had been. Minutes? Hours? Time had just stopped. And I started to think about all the awful things that could have happened. Maybe Mum couldn't find Jade. Maybe she had got lost in the smoke. Maybe Jade was stuck in there. Or hurt, or maybe she was . . . I couldn't bring myself to think the last thing so instead I started making promises. I promised that if Mum and Jade were OK, I would never be bad again.

I could feel the closest twin's fingers digging into my hand. His shoulders were shaking. 'I'm sorry, I'm sorry, I'm so sorry,' he muttered.

I promise that if Mum and Jade are OK, I will never make fun of Grandma again.

'Why did you leave Henry?' the other twin roared at his brother, making the whole car shake.

I promise I will try harder at shrinking, Dad. Dad, just make sure they're OK. Please, Dad, please.

And then I saw it. Shadows moving in the smoke. Coming closer . . . and closer. I was screaming at them, and almost beat through the glass. Out of the smoke came Mum, almost bent to her knees. And then behind her, her arms wrapped around Mum's shoulders was Jade, her face sooty, her green eyes swollen. I had never wanted to see my sister so badly. Henry trailed behind, hanging on to the back of Jade's T-shirt.

They collapsed into a panting heap on the tarmac by the side of the car. Mum wiped sweat from her forehead and unlocked the car door. I flung myself at her and Jade.

'I tried to save the furniture,' Jade squeaked. 'But I couldn't find the way through the smoke.'

'Doesn't matter. You're safe now,' Mum croaked. 'I've got you. I've got both my girls.'

'I'm so sorry, I'm so, so sorry, Mum. We thought we could put it out, but then the spray paints exploded and we couldn't stop it.' Jade gulped. 'The furniture's ruined, Mum. I've ruined everything.'

'Knickers to the furniture. I have you,' Mum said, hugging Jade. 'And I have you,' she said, pulling me in.

As the sirens got closer we held on to each other like we would never let go.

Twenty

Me, Mum and Jade slept for a very long time. By the time we woke up, everyone knew about what had happened. Henry and the twins' parents came over to thank Mum and brought flowers. Then Bobby came over to see if I was all right and brought chocolates. Then Grandma and Ed came over and insisted on making us dinner. Secretly we all wished everyone would go away. We were so tired. Even talking seemed exhausting. But Grandma decided to do enough talking for all of us.

'You let little Sydney drive! What were you thinking?'

'If it wasn't for her, I don't think we would have made it in time.'

'And then you went in after them! Amy, why didn't you wait for the fire brigade?'

'Mum was brilliant. She saved Jade and even Hairy Henry.'

'But it was reckless and dangerous and—'

Ed interrupted Grandma. 'And I don't think I've ever been prouder to know someone in my whole life.'

'You are a stupid, stubborn . . . brave woman. But if you ever do anything like that again, so help me God.'

Mum held out her arms for a hug, but Grandma just raised an eyebrow.

'This is silk and it'll wrinkle,' she said, turning away for a private sniffle.

Mum sighed. 'I'm afraid all our furniture's ruined though. Oh, Ed, I'm sorry – only three days before the competition.'

I thought of the furniture, all Mum's and Ed's hard work, black and charred and misshapen, poking up through the collapsed roof like broken bones. All our hopes, gone. And a dark, tiny part of me wished it wasn't Jade Mum had saved but the furniture.

Then Grandma started up again. 'You were ruining your hands with all that manual labour,

Amy. To think I went to all that trouble to get you an office job.'

Mum shrugged. 'I guess you're going to get your way now, because if there was ever a sign that I should let it go, that was it.'

Ed let go of Mum's hand and everyone fell quiet. I tried not to imagine Mum in her sad little grey suits forever. I tried not to imagine our shop in London cold and empty. I tried not to imagine staying in Portsmouth. Grandma made us something more to eat, but I couldn't eat a thing. I was so tired I just wanted to sleep.

That night I slipped into my cold bed without looking at Jade.

There was a part of me that was so angry at her that it felt as if I was on fire, burning to a cinder. It was all her fault, all of it. She had made me miserable. She had abandoned me and had destroyed everything of Mum's and Ed's. Worst of all, she had got us stuck here in Portsmouth with no way out.

So when Jade crept into my bed and put her arms around me, something I had wished she would do since the moment we had got here, instead of hugging her back, I twisted away quickly like an otter and thumped her in the face with an elbow. I didn't even think to do it. But the moment I did, I realized how unstoppably mad I was — my insides were burning, and no shrinking exercise or words of Dad's could stop me wanting to murder my big sister.

Jade fell out of the bed with a thump. When I saw her sitting on the floor holding her bloody nose, the fire inside me raged out of control. I threw myself at her, and even though she's twice my size I had her pinned in a matter of seconds. My fingers dug into the soft flannel of her pyjama collar and I lifted one hand and slapped her right across the cheek. It took only a moment for a bright red mark to come up. Jade made a little gaspy noise and squirmed out from under me. She didn't look so fierce any more. In fact, she looked scared. Maybe I would have cared, maybe I would have stopped, but I wasn't Sydney any more, I was a savage burning thing, an out-of-control fire of fury and revenge, so I lifted my hand to hit her again. Jade bellowed, 'Enough!' and kneed me hard in my lady parts. I suddenly didn't feel like a

Wild Thing any more as I rolled over, clutching my knees.

'Don't make me kick your ass,' Jade muttered, but I could tell all the fight had gone out of her too.

We lay on the floor panting.

'You sucker-punched me, you cheat,' Jade said, scrambling to get to her feet, but when she realized her nose was still bleeding she gave up halfway and sat up against the bedroom wall.

I looked up at her as she held her nose and looked back at me between her fingers.

'I didn't mean to kick you down there,' Jade said, giggling. 'I guess that makes us even.'

I got on my hands and knees and sat against the wall next to her. 'Don't count on it,' I muttered.

'I wanted to thank you for coming and saving me, but now I'm not so sure.'

'I shouldn't have bothered.'

'No, you probably shouldn't have.'

'I hate you.'

'I know,' she said, slipping an arm around me and pulling me close. My face pressed up against the soft material of her pyjamas and I wasn't mad at her any more. Jade no longer seemed like a fearless stranger. She was my sister and we were just tired.

'I'm sorry, little thing,' she whispered in my ear, and I could still smell smoke in her hair.

'Can we go to bed and forget about it?' I said.

But Jade just sat there.

'When I close my eyes, I still see the fire,' she mumbled.

So I climbed into Jade's bed with her and pulled the cover over us. I waited until her eyes had stopped flickering behind her eyelids before I tried to fall asleep. But I couldn't. So I stared at the bumps on the ceiling, trying to imagine them as stars swirling above us. I worried the moment I shut my eyes I would see it too. That smoke would fill my dreams. That Mum would be endlessly running into a blaze of orange. But when I finally did fall asleep I didn't see the fire, I saw London. Not Big Ben or the Tower of London, not Buckingham Palace or even Harrods, but my London. Narrow streets, dirty tube stations, the little park at the end of our road lined by iron railings, the terraced houses where Harriet and Anna lived. Miss Peters' pink shop and *our* shop, with its big window and gold-lettered sign. And above that our old flat with its pointed red-brick roof and wonky chimney stack.

It felt so real I could almost touch it. Almost.

Twenty-one

Somehow over summer half-term everyone at school had heard about the fire, too. Before I'd even arrived for the first day back, everyone on the playground had been talking about it. Bobby had been the source of all knowledge and had a gang of girls around him asking every question imaginable, like:

Was anyone mangled or burned?

Did my mum really run in and carry out three people on her back?

Was it true I started the fire to get back at my sister?

Bobby was grinning from ear to ear when I got in. He had never felt so popular.

'Well, if it isn't the celebrity,' he said, slapping me on the back.

'What do you mean?'

'Look around, mate.'

All around me children stared and pointed. It was like walking through a giant game of Chinese whispers. Even Alison and her gang were watching me, their eyes wide with a look between impressed and slightly terrified. Alison gave me a little nod as she strode across the playground to the school building.

'See?' Bobby said. 'You're the talk of the school. Everyone wants to know about the fire. It's about the most interesting thing that's happened all year.'

I looked at him, but I didn't know what to say.

He smiled and said, 'Well, apart from when Mrs Pervis went berserk during a music lesson and chucked a recorder at one of the Year Threes.'

As we followed everyone into school, I was starting to wonder about all these tales about Mrs Pervis. People had got it so twisted up and wrong about the fire. Believing everything, from me deliberately trapping my sister in the lock-ups, to my mum single-handedly rescuing a whole football team's worth of people from a full-on inferno.

So maybe some of the rumours about Mrs Pervis weren't entirely true either.

One thing was true though; she was still a complete crazy. So when before class she invited me to come into her Head of Year office, I was half expecting to get a recorder, or a trumpet, or maybe even a drum kit lobbed at me? It was bad enough half the school thought I was some sort of fire starter. Who knew what Psycho Pervis thought?

I was so nervous I thought I would have to dash off to the loo while I was outside waiting to be asked in. I tried to do a shrinking exercise to calm myself down. I closed my eyes and tried to concentrate everything into doing the *'Flickering Monk'*, imagining myself disappearing for a few seconds and coming back smaller, disappearing for a few more seconds and getting even tinier. But it didn't feel right; it just felt like I was holding my breath and shaking my arms.

Since the fire, since nearly losing Jade and knowing that I would never go home again, I felt as if I had lost all of my shrinking abilities, and I couldn't hear Dad's voice any more either. I couldn't even hear my own. My head felt empty. There were no plans or ideas, no happy thoughts, no good memories, just blank space. I felt like I was disappearing, and I wasn't the only one. On our first day back to school, even Mum, who never let anything get her down, had woken up tired and red-eyed. She hadn't gone down to see Ed in the morning either. Instead she had put on her vilest, greyest suit, and pushed aside her usual Marmite toast and banana breakfast for plain black coffee.

'Grandma's right – we need to grow up. We need a new start. I'm so sorry I've been letting you girls down. But from now on everything's going to change, I promise you,' she said before we left for school.

Jade just nodded at us and went to the bathroom to cut out her pink, and now slightly singed, strand of hair.

But I didn't want a new start. And I certainly didn't want everything to change. That was the problem. What we needed was things to go back to the way they used to be. When it was Jade, Mum and me against the world. When we had our shop with all its memories of Dad.

All this was swirling around in my head when Mrs Pervis finally called me into her office.

'Sydney, we like to speak to some of our students in special situations,' she said, studying me. 'Or after they have experienced trying events, just to check in and make sure they are doing OK. In fact, we have a group for our special students.'

But I knew there wasn't anything special or different about me any more. I was just a stupid troll like everyone else. I thought about how disappointed Dad would be in me. Or maybe he wouldn't. I just didn't know any more. I hated Mrs Pervis for confusing me like this. I wished I could use my powers on her. I wished I could shrink her down, down and down. Until she was the size of a butterfly and the smallest breeze would blow her away. But I knew I couldn't. I was helpless. And then suddenly this feeling came over me. The same one that had come over me when I had fought Jade. I could feel this Wild Thing stirring inside me.

'I'm not in a "special" situation and I don't need any stupid "special" group. And most of all,' I shouted, 'I don't need you having a go at me any more!'

It wasn't me speaking any more, it was the Wild Thing. And the Wild Thing was angry. So angry that before I knew it I was yelling straight into Mrs Pervis's face. My arms shot out in front of me and pushed all the books off her desk.

Mrs Pervis gasped. 'Sydney!'

As quickly as the Wild Thing had come, it went. It deserted me, leaving me to face the consequences of its actions all alone.

Mrs Pervis pulled herself up and stared at me in a way I had never seen. She had a shocked expression, a bit like Jade's after the fire. Normally Mrs Pervis was terrifying. Everyone was scared of her. You just nodded your head and did what you were told. Sometimes someone might cry a bit, but no one – no one – ever yelled at Mrs Pervis, and no one would have ever dared push her books over.

I could only imagine what was going to happen to me. Perhaps she would expel me, or maybe have me taken away to the 'special group', never to be seen again.

But she didn't do any of that. Instead she continued to stare at me for a few seconds, and then she laughed. It started off as a giggle and then turned into full-on laughter. And her laugh wasn't like any ordinary laugh. It was almost like music. It went up and down, you could almost sing to it. And when she finished, she grinned. But not in the sly way Jade does, or in the embarrassed way Grandma does. Mrs Pervis smiled in a way that made her eyes crinkle and her face completely change. She looked almost friendly. It was the most surprising thing I could have ever imagined.

'Sydney, dear,' she said, 'would you mind picking up those books?'

I nodded madly and gathered them all up into my arms and returned them in a heap to her desk.

'Well, as enjoyable as this little chat was, Sydney, I think we should return to class, don't you?'

And I nodded frantically again.

'You do know though, don't you,' Mrs Pervis added, opening the door to her office, 'that you can always tell me if there are any problems, special or not.'

But by now her face had returned to normal. The hard lines had come back and the steely glint was back in her eyes. I didn't feel like talking to her any more, so I just mumbled 'OK' as I followed her back to class.

Bobby's face lit up when I walked into the room.

'You survived,' he whispered when I sat down.

'Course I did,' I said more bravely than I felt.

'Many who go in don't come back,' Bobby said in an ominous voice.

I couldn't tell if he was being serious or not.

'So what was it like inside the beast's den?'

I didn't know quite how to explain what had happened, to him or even to myself, so I just said, 'I almost didn't make it.'

Bobby nodded solemnly and started explaining what I'd missed in the recycling project the class was doing.

'Did you know there's this artist who built a whole island out of recycled bags and bottles? It has a real house, and even has flowers and mangroves growing on it. And there's this lake that's—'

'Robert!' Mrs Pervis growled. 'Do you want me to take fifteen minutes from your lunch break before we even begin the lesson?'

The funny thing was that even though me and Bobby had to carry on our conversation in a whisper, and even though Mrs Pervis went on snapping and terrifying everyone the same way she always did in class, the funny thing was, I didn't feel scared of her any more.

Twenty-two

I couldn't risk the Wild Thing escaping again so I did some shrinking routines before bed that night. I curled myself up into a tight little ball until I could hardly breathe. I imagined my bones and muscles being squished up as I whispered:

From my head, to my feet, to my toes, to my knees,
Keep all of me small if you please.
I need to fit into tree houses, secret passages and child
*   swings with ease.*
From my head, to my feet, to my toes, to my knees,
Keep all of me small if you please . . .

I muttered it into my pillow again and again and again until the words didn't make sense any more. I tried so hard to make them sound right, but

I must have fallen asleep. When I woke up it was pitch black. I could hear Jade sleeping. She made these little breathy sounds and I watched the dark lump in her bed rise and fall. I wished I could go back to sleep, but I couldn't stop thinking about our shop and how we would never see it again. I so badly wanted to talk about it to someone, but I knew it would make Mum too sad and Jade too angry. So I slipped out of bed and wandered into the kitchen. I tried to sit on the littlest bear chair from the set Mum had made us, but I was too big. I kept sliding off. So I sat in Mum's middle-sized chair, but that was a bit too small now as well. I scooted over to Jade's big chair and folded my head into my arms and cried. All the shrinking cream was gone and none of my shrinking exercises seemed to be working any more.

What would Dad think? I tried to picture his face but I couldn't; my imagination would only conjure up Alviss, the master-craftsman dwarf who had been tricked by Thor and turned to stone. I saw his frozen stone face out among the trees. Dad's stories always had so much detail you could almost reach out and touch them. So when I closed my eyes I could imagine the great big red pines, their long tree trunks heading up into the sky and Alviss's little stone body hidden among them. I could feel the damp leaves of the forest floor under my feet, hear the snap of twigs as I brushed through branches. Then I could see the first rays of the sun appearing from behind the mountain. I knew if its rays caught me I would be turned to stone too. So into the trees I ran as fast as I could. But the forest's branches kept reaching out for me and ivy crawled around my body, pulling me down, down, down. I tried to untangle myself but their grip tightened around me. And then the sun rose through the trees. I felt my fingertips harden, then my hand, then my arm, and then . . . I woke with a jolt, still in Jade's chair, my head in a little pool of saliva on the table. Sunlight filled the kitchen and I heard Mum getting up: the creak of the floorboards, the click of the light switch. So I rushed back into my room and pulled on my school things.

'You're up and ready early,' Mum said when I appeared in the kitchen. 'I thought I would make you and Jade a proper breakfast. Eggs, bacon, toast, maybe even some of those little baby mushrooms you like?' she offered, cracking an egg into the pan.

But I shook my head. I couldn't have eaten a thing. I felt as if my insides really had been turned to stone.

Jade came into the kitchen then, sniffing the bacon-filled air.

'How about you, Jade? I'm making the bacon crispy just the way you like it.'

Jade shrugged. 'I think I'm becoming a vegetarian.'

'Of course you are,' Mum said, rolling her eyes at me. 'Well, more bacon for me.'

'I wouldn't mind the eggs and mushrooms though,' Jade added.

'Have some toast at least, Sydney. I can't send you to school with an empty tummy.'

But I didn't want to go to school. I wanted to tell Mum how I had been turned to stone. How I couldn't see Dad's face any more, how I wanted to go back home to London so badly it hurt. But I didn't.

At school Bobby could see I just wanted to be

left alone, so he made a game out of avoiding everyone. We pretended we were ninjas and that no one could see us and then at lunch we went and hid in the teachers' car park.

'You want to tell me what's wrong?' he asked as we wriggled up against the side of a hot car.

'Nothing,' I said, scuffing my feet in the gravel.

'That's what my dad always says. He says we shouldn't talk about our problems all the time. But Mum says he bottles everything up and that's why he gets migraines.'

But it all felt too big to tell Bobby. I didn't know where to start. When me, Anna and Harriet couldn't talk about something that was upsetting us, we would write it down in a special notebook and pass it to each other to read and write things back in. Sometimes we wrote these really long stories about how this one girl had said something really mean and then when we read them back later they seemed so stupid. But since I'd moved away, I'd only spoken to them on the phone a few times, but it wasn't the same. We couldn't find very much to say now we didn't see each other every day, and I couldn't do the notebook thing with Bobby so I just drew a sad face in the gravel with the tip of my shoe.

Bobby jumped up. 'I've got an idea, I'll be right back,' he yelled as he ran off towards our classroom. When he came back his arms were full of rolls of coloured art paper. He tipped them out on to the ground in front of me. And from his pockets he pulled out big fat marker pens, the kind that give you headaches if you sniff them.

'Draw it,' he said, and he unrolled the paper and drew a wobbly stick figure of me, with long flicky brown hair and giant boots. Then he drew himself as a big blob with a tiny head covered in spiky black hair.

'That's not what we look like,' I said, laughing.

'All right, you do it,' Bobby said, shoving a marker into my hand.

I squinted at Bobby and started drawing his face. Bright blue eyes, a giant grin, thick curly black hair. Then I kept on drawing. I gave him a cape and a tablet with the Wikipedia page on it.

'I guess that's better than mine.' Bobby shrugged but I could tell he was pleased. 'Do yourself now.'

So I drew myself with a huge bush of messy red and brown hair, big brown eyes and I gave myself the skull T-shirt Jade had made me wear to the funfair and sparkly red buckle shoes that I had once seen in Miss Peters' shop window and lightning-bolt earrings just like Jade's.

'You look badass.' Bobby nodded approvingly. 'But I'd better get some of these pens back before the end of lunch.'

But once I had started I couldn't stop. I spread out a fresh roll of art paper and started drawing. First the letter Miss Peters had sent us about the furniture competition. Then the prize money as a heap of gold coins. I drew our shop, with its wonky roof and big gold sign. Then I drew London, with all the things people recognize, and then I added in the little park down our old road and Harriet's house and Mr Wu's fish and chip shop. Then I drew all of Mum's furniture, the chaise longue, the leather armchair, even the iron headboard. Bobby kept pointing at my drawing, asking, 'Who's that? What's happening now?' So as I drew I had to explain about the competition and how we had wanted to get the shop back. Then I drew the fire in great big spiky orange pen strokes. Then Mum pulling Jade and Hairy Henry out of it and all the furniture lying around them as burnt sticks. It took all lunchtime. But when I was finally finished I drew a great big red cross through our shop and scribbled out London. I rubbed right through the page, erasing Big Ben; my red double-decker buses became red blobs and London Bridge faded away under a mess of brown marker. I hadn't even noticed that Bobby had tried to stop me scribbling out my drawings. He had ink marks all over his hands.

'Why did you do that?' he asked.

'Because I'm never going back. I'm never going back to London. I'm never going home!' I yelled.

'It's not so bad here. You've got the sea and the funfair and—'

'I hate it. I hate everything about it. I just want to go home!'

'And me, you've got me here,' Bobby said in a tiny voice.

But I didn't say anything, even though I could see Bobby hang his head. We both went very quiet and then Bobby picked up my drawing and tore it up and let the pieces fly into the air. He stomped off. His footsteps made angry crunching noises all the way across the car park and back into our school.

I tried to apologize to Bobby, but he ignored me the rest of the day. He pretended he was still a ninja and that no one could see him, even me. Alison and her gang noticed and kept sniggering and whispering to each other.

'Aw, your boyfriend don't love you any more?' Alison taunted.

I narrowed my eyes and gave her the look Jade gives Mum when she asks her to take the bins out. It worked too, because Alison's friend poked her and said, 'Stop it, Ali – you know she starts fires.' And they all nudged their chairs away from me. I felt quite powerful as the 'fire starter'. So powerful in fact that in art later that day every time I wanted the coloured pens or scissors or paper Alison's table was using, I would point menacingly and wiggle my fingers as if I could summon a terrible fire demon, until one of Alison's friends gave me what I wanted. By the end of the day I had all the high-lighters and glitter pens.

My new notoriety didn't impress Bobby though. He turned his chair so he had his back to me for most of the afternoon. I wanted to take everything I'd said back, but I couldn't. At the end of the day I walked home alone.

Twenty-three

I worried the whole weekend about Bobby being mad at me. I worried about it so much that by Monday I had made myself ill. Mum had to call Grandma to come and look after me. Jade tried to be 'ill' too. She sat at the end of my bed and did a feeble cough. 'Oh, I feel quite faint,' she said, putting a palm to her forehead.

'I'd better pack the smelling salts then,' Mum said as she pulled Jade out of the door with her.

'Feel better, Syd. You don't want to waste a day off by actually being ill,' Jade yelled on the way out.

Grandma sat on my bed and patted my head. 'You do look a bit peaky,' she said, pinching her face up.

I couldn't tell if she was worried about me or if

she was worried I might be sick on her. But I didn't really care. I just wanted to stay in bed. I imagined it as a little island floating off into the wide blue sea. Somewhere far away from Portsmouth, somewhere far away where I didn't have to think about Bobby, or our shop, or Dad, or shrinking. I screwed up my eyes and pulled the covers over my head.

By lunchtime the house smelt of delicious chicken soup and herby dumplings. Grandma had been cooking and I was a little bit tempted to come off my secret island. Just a little bit, but not quite enough. Eventually Grandma swept into my room.

'Sydney, enough of this bed nonsense. Up, up, and get some food in yourself.'

'I'm ill,' I whined, pulling the bedcovers tighter over my head.

'Well, I guess if you're that ill, I'll have to call the doctor then.'

I hate the doctor's — just sitting in the waiting room freaks me out, so I got up.

'Fine.' I trudged into the kitchen.

Grandma shook out a big white napkin and tucked it into my pyjama top. I hadn't known we had napkins. I wondered if Grandma had brought them from her house.

'Eat your soup, you'll feel better.'

I took a little sip off my spoon, pretending it was horrible, even though it was hot and salty and delicious.

'Your mother's worried about you, you know. She's worried about both you and Jade.'

But I didn't reply. I just spooned dumplings into my mouth.

'I hope you're not keeping secrets, Sydney.' Grandma stared at me, her blue eyes drilling deep. I felt as if she could see right inside me. See all my shrinking techniques, and how much I missed Dad. Then she straightened in her chair and I was sure she would say exactly what I had been thinking.

'Is something the matter with your school?' she asked.

I sighed with relief. 'I had a fight with my friend. Now he won't speak to me.'

'Well, it certainly won't be your last fight with a boy. I promise he'll forgive you sooner than you think,' Grandma said, giving me a knowing nod.

Grandma was right, because as soon as school was over Bobby showed up at the flat.

'I just came to see if you were OK,' he said, scuffing a leg back and forth over our welcome mat.

I nodded. 'I'm OK.'

'Good.' He sniffed and then turned to leave.

'Wait! I'm sorry, I'm really sorry.'

'Well, in or out?' Grandma yelled from the kitchen. 'You're letting all the heat out.'

Bobby shrugged and followed me into mine and Jade's room.

'I didn't mean what I said. I mean, I meant some of it, but not the bit about hating everything. I don't hate you, Bobby – you're one of my best friends.'

'Well, I wouldn't say you were one of my best friends, but you're all right,' Bobby said, grinning.

I elbowed him and he elbowed me back.

'I was so worried you would never speak to me again,' I said.

'Would you have forgotten me if you had moved back?'

'No! I would have called you all the time. And

you could have come up and stayed. Me and Jade had our own rooms, so you could have slept in mine . . .' I trailed off.

'Good,' Bobby said. 'Because I have a plan.'

Bobby's plan was so simple and yet so genius I wondered why I hadn't thought of it myself. Even though he knew it would mean me moving back to London and him having to deal with Alison and her gang on his own again, he explained everything in the way people do when they're really excited about something. With big arms waving everywhere and with a voice that gets higher and higher as it goes on.

'Well, do you remember that man who made a whole island out of plastic bottles and bags and rubbish? I started looking it up and there's all these other people who do stuff like that − it's called "upcycling". You can take anything and make something new out of it.'

'But we don't have time to make something. It took Ed and Mum months to make that last lot.'

'You don't need to. You just take what you already have and make it better.' Bobby started digging about in his bag. 'I brought some pictures.'

In one picture a man had turned a lawnmower into a fancy plant pot with flowers pouring out from the top of it and vines wrapped around the handles. In another someone had turned a bathtub into a sofa just like the one out of Mum's and my favourite old film. Someone had even made a chandelier from old jam jars. But what really caught my eye was a full-length oval mirror that a woman had decorated with recycled green glass made to look like ivy twisting around the frame. It looked just like something out of one of Dad's stories.

'This is amazing,' I breathed. 'But we don't have a mirror, or a lawnmower, or any of this stuff.'

'No, but you have your trunk.'

We both looked at my treasure chest with its curved wooden lid and its shiny brass lock.

'My dad made that,' I whispered.

'Well, he would want you to use it if it would help you get back home,' Bobby said, and I knew he was right.

We had talked so long that we hadn't noticed Mum and Jade come home, or Grandma leave. Mum rang Bobby's parents to let them know where he was and ask if it was OK for him to stay for dinner. She even made a special effort and cooked chicken and chips. But it wasn't nearly as nice as Grandma's soup. Me and Bobby had to hide all the burnt chips under our plates. I didn't mind though because inside my head I was making a plan, a secret plan.

Twenty-four

That night, a forest sprang up in my bedroom. But it wasn't one I dreamed of, it was one I painted. With the art set Miss Peters had given me I painted the treasure chest with the forest from Dad's stories. By the light of my torch I drew orange and brown leaves across the bottom and long tall trees up the sides and a brilliant gold sun and little silver birds swirling across the lid. I had almost finished it when Jade woke up.

'What – are you trying to blind me? It's the middle of the night!' she bellowed as she flipped the bedcovers off, leaped out of bed and grabbed the torch.

But then she saw the treasure chest, the top glittering with little winged birds.

'Wow, Syd! What is this?'

I tried to explain the plan. To take our old stuff and make it new. I got out the photos Bobby had given me and showed her. I wished Bobby had been there to explain it properly, because Jade kept asking a lot of questions I didn't know the answers to. In the end she seemed to understand though. She nodded. 'We could do the three bear chairs and table too.'

'Yeah!' I yelled and Jade nudged me. 'Yeah,' I whispered.

'But I still don't think it's enough, and the competition's in two weeks,' Jade pointed out.

'I guess we'll need help then,' I whispered as we crawled back into our beds.

Getting everyone together wasn't easy. We had to wait until the weekend before Mum was properly free, and then Jade refused to go and get Ed. But Bobby came over and organized everyone.

When everyone was finally sitting down, I pulled out my treasure chest.

Mum gasped. 'It's beautiful!'

'It's the forest from one of Dad's stories,' I said.

Mum hugged me. 'He'd love it,' she whispered in my ear.

'It's for the competition,' I said, wriggling away, a bit embarrassed.

'Oh, Sydney, it's lovely, it truly is. But we can't just show one piece.'

'But it's not until next Sunday.'

'It took your mum and me months to make the last pieces,' Ed said.

'But that's the thing,' Bobby piped up. 'You don't need to make new things. You have everything you already need. You just need to make it better.' He launched into his whole speech; he even passed around the pictures explaining how each one had been made.

'We can do the bear chairs and the table too,' Jade added.

Mum had fallen very quiet. Me, Bobby, Jade and Ed looked at her.

'I thought I'd put this all behind me. I thought I was done.' She groaned as she rubbed her forehead.

My heart sank, Ed crinkled his brow and Bobby sank to the floor.

Only Jade faced Mum, her hands on her hips. 'It's my fault. It's all my fault,' my sister said. 'But you can't give up. I'll help . . . I'll even help Ed.'

Mum sighed a deep sigh, and then looked up. I noticed a mischievous glint in her eye.

'What are you all sitting around for then? We have a lot of work to do.'

We all rushed into action. Mum and Ed spent the rest of the morning sanding down the three bear chairs and the matching table. Then they started painting. I could tell it was going to take all day because Mum was using the tiny brushes she uses for the fancy delicate work. So me, Bobby and Jade rushed around getting more paints and brushes. We even made a fancy lunch of soup and hot cheese rolls and fresh fruit salad. It was dinner time when Mum and Ed finished, and our kitchen and living room were covered in paint and sawdust.

'What do you think?' Mum said, stepping back.

The table was now painted with a world of streams and rivers and forests, and running through the middle was a mountain range.

'Look,' Mum said as she pointed to the rocky slopes, 'this is where Anouk and her giant family lived.' Then she pointed across the other side of the table to the forest. 'This is Tomas's dwarf village.' Then I understood that this was Dad's story about how average-height people came to be. On the backrest of the big chair Mum had painted Anouk the giant, and on the little chair she had painted Tomas the dwarf. On the middle chair she had painted them together, holding hands after God had heard their prayers and made them average size.

'I think it's fantastic,' I breathed.

'I learned from the best,' Mum said, winking at me.

That night we had dinner sitting on the floor, but nobody minded. I kept looking up at Anouk and Tomas, and for the first time I felt as if everything might be all right. Bobby nudged me as we ate Ed's delicious mushroom risotto. 'Your mum is amazing,' he whispered.

When Bobby came over the next day he was all smiles. He had brought his dad's hammer and waved it proudly.

'My dad said if I'm going to learn to build stuff I can come over every weekend,' he said. Then Ed turned up lugging a dusty old rocking chair. It looked like something out of a cowboy movie. It was huge with sled-like rockers covered in splinters. 'It was my grandpa's,' he said proudly. 'What do you think?'

I watched a spider crawl over the seat and said, 'I think it needs work.'

No one quite knew what to do with Ed's rocking chair. Jade tried painting it but the paint just peeled off. Ed tried sanding it, but it just made it splinter more. Mum went to take it apart, but Ed stopped her.

'I can't let you do that. This is the chair my grandpa told me stories about his travels in. I would sit on his lap and he'd talk for hours about all the bears and wolves and eagles he'd seen.'

We all stood staring at the chair for a long time. I tried to imagine Ed as a little boy, but I couldn't picture him as anything but bald.

'What if we covered it in something?' Bobby said finally.

'I know just the thing,' Jade yelled, and she rushed off to Mum's bedroom. When she reappeared she was holding up the fur coat Miss Peters had given Mum. 'Let's make it a real bear chair,' she said, stroking the coat.

It took all that Sunday to turn Ed's chair into the bear chair. Ed and Jade took the fur coat apart and then cut it up and stapled pieces over the back of the chair. Then they covered the arms of the chair, but by then we had run out of fur coat! So Mum and me made a seat pillow out of foam and covered it in brown leather. The rocker part was the trickiest though; it was so dirty and scratched. Bobby and Ed spent a long time cleaning it and rubbing it with a special wax. By the time it dried it almost looked brand new. To finish it off, Ed put little leather claws on the ends of the rockers. Then we all had several turns trying it out.

Afterwards Mum said, 'It's good. But something's missing.'

'It's not really the centrepiece we need,' Ed added.

'We need something else,' Bobby agreed.

'What we need is your grandma and her old sofa,' Mum exclaimed, and rushed off to make a phone call.

Then Ed took the bus over to Grandma's. He returned with a two-seater sofa wedged in the back of her Morris Minor, and with Grandma herself driving. She didn't look happy when Mum explained what we intended to do with her sofa. Me and Jade and Bobby watched from the window. Grandma's arms swung in big circles and Mum looked even smaller than usual. We didn't have to hear what they were saying. We knew Grandma was telling Mum off for not wanting a real job. We could only imagine how many French words were in there too. Ed came in after a while and then Grandma's arms stopped looping the loop and Mum called Ed back out. Then the three of them carried the sofa into the building and up the stairs. When they finally got it into the flat, Grandma collapsed into it.

'This is a nice couch. Grey velvet,' she puffed. 'I got it from Laura Ashley before they went downmarket. It was expensive too. Well, it would have been, but I got it on sale.' She sighed. 'God forbid you use it to sit on! No, no, you want to wreck it for some arty show.'

She pushed herself up and stood in the middle of

the room with her hands on her hips. 'I guess you have what you need now.'

Jade and I looked at one another. Then Mum looked at Grandma.

'Actually, Mum, what I really need is your help.'

Twenty-five

The thing that I've learned about grandmas is this. They can't resist if you ask them for help. They just have to. Once Mum explained what we were doing – bringing our family stories to life and that we couldn't do it without her – Grandma's face softened.

'So, what are you going to do with the couch then?' she asked.

'Actually, Mum, that's where we need your help. You're the expert seamstress – what do you think we should do?'

Grandma looked at the couch and then at Mum and smiled. 'I know just the thing,' she said. 'But it's going to take a lot of work. I'll have to work every day and you'll all have to help in the evenings if we are to get it done in time.'

We all started the very next day after Mum got home from work.

'Right, we have a lot of work to do,' Grandma announced, striding into the kitchen. Her hair was pinned up into a yellow silk scarf, her cream jumper neatly tucked into her navy trousers. Even Work Grandma looked amazing.

'I need you to gather all the fabric, all the old bits of material you can find. Anything and everything – I need it here.'

We all just stared at her.

'*Vite, vite, allez, allez!* We don't have time to waste.'

We rushed off. From the cupboard I pulled out the moon pyjamas that didn't fit me any more. Jade grabbed her black T-shirt with the silver lightning bolt. She had last worn it on the night of the fire and it still smelt of smoke. Mum found our old velvet curtains from London still packed in a box. Ed came back with a pile of cushions; some had sailing boats on them, others had birds. Grandma looked at everything admiringly.

'This is perfect. Just perfect.'

'But what are you going to do with it all?' I asked.

Grandma looked at Mum and Mum looked back, smiling like she suddenly understood.

'We are going to make a memory quilt,' they both said.

I wasn't even allowed to ask what that was, because no sooner had they said it than Grandma's old sewing machine sprang into action. The sound of it whirring went on all week.

Actually, making the quilt was something only Mum and Grandma could do as they were the only ones who could sew. So after school me and Bobby hunted for thread and fabric at the local charity shop. Ed made dinner. Although half the time Mum and Grandma were too busy to stop and eat so Jade made them sandwiches, making sure to cut off the crusts and cut them into four 'petite' triangles the way Grandma liked them.

In the evenings Grandma and Mum chatted and laughed. Sometimes Grandma told Mum off, and Mum would huff out of the room yelling she was done, only to return a minute or two later. But the really surprising thing was that after a couple of days Mum and Grandma went silent. Me and Jade had never seen them like it before. And somehow they each knew exactly what the other needed. They passed each other scraps of fabrics cut into shapes that looked like they could never fit together, and then they managed to make it join like a massive confusing jigsaw puzzle.

On Saturday the sound of the sewing machine stopped. Mum and Grandma stepped back to admire their work. The result was a patchwork quilt in all kinds of colours and fabrics. Some I recognized: the red patches were from our velvet curtains, the birds from Ed's cushions. In the top right-hand corner was Jade's lightning bolt, on the other side were the moons from my pyjamas. It was all knitted together with beautiful gold stitching that seemed to shine.

'So this is a memory quilt?' I asked.

'Well, it's a memory couch,' Mum said as she and Ed tucked and then pinned the quilt over Grandma's couch.

Grandma spent the rest of day supervising the sewing of the different covering pieces. The memory quilt was fitted over the back of the couch, while the rest of our red velvet curtains were made into covers to fit over the arms. The grey velvet seat cushions were left. It became an amazing multicoloured patchwork couch. One of a kind, just like the things Mum and Dad used to make.

The morning of the show, we all gathered to watch Ed and Jade load the couch into our newly repaired truck. But there was so much stuff that Ed had also borrowed a trailer. Jade kept bossing Ed around, telling him how everything should fit. It took them ages to work out what should go where, and once they did decide they started arguing about when to push and lift the furniture. I couldn't pay attention though. I kept waiting for Bobby to show up. I watched the clouds drift above and squinted my eyes, trying to see shapes in them.

'Hey.' Bobby waved as he strode around the corner.

'I didn't think you were going to make it,' I said, smiling.

'Actually I just came to wish you luck.'

'You're not coming with us?'

Bobby shook his head. 'I want you to win, I really do. But . . .' He couldn't finish.

He didn't have to. We both knew he wanted me to stay. I thought about taking his hand, but instead we both just stared up at the sky.

'Bobby . . .' I started to say.

But he just patted me on the back hard and grunted, 'Good luck, I really mean it.' Then he was gone.

I watched the clouds drift apart. Just for a moment I was a little sad at the thought of leaving Portsmouth.

'Is Bobby not coming with us?' Mum asked.

'No, he just can't,' I said, staring hard at my shoes.

'That's a shame,' she said, patting me on the shoulder. We watched Ed and Jade carefully load the rest of the furniture into the truck. First the table and chairs, followed by the rocking bear chair and finally my treasure chest.

Mum put her arm around Grandma's waist and they smiled at each other.

'It's *magnifique*,' Grandma said in her most French accent. Then she shook her head. 'Actually it's just plain old wonderful.'

'We have a spare space now. Do you want to come with us?' Mum asked her.

'I wouldn't want to be a burden.'

'I could use a good seamstress, in case any stitching comes loose,' Mum said, giving me and Jade a little wink. We all knew that Mum could repair just about anything on her own.

Grandma saw us smirking and muttered, 'Well, if you really think I'm that indispensable.'

'Yeah, Mum, joking aside, I really do need you.'

Grandma's face flushed with delight. 'Well, it is a good excuse to wear my pearls.'

Twenty-six

The ride up to London was nothing like our trip to Portsmouth four months before. Everyone was filled with excitement. The newly fixed truck buzzed with it, and I had to sit on my hands to keep from fidgeting. Mum kept catching our glances in the rear-view mirror as she drove and giggled nervously. Grandma sat bolt upright next to Mum, her eyes gleaming. She was quite enjoying her new role as head seamstress. Me, Jade and Ed sat squished up in the back. But amazingly Jade and Ed seemed to be getting on.

'I think it's time I learned to play an instrument,' he said to her. 'Do you think you could teach me guitar? I wouldn't even mind learning that song you wrote about me – it was pretty good.'

Jade turned red and shuffled her feet. 'OK,' she

muttered, 'I suppose I could. But you'll probably be crap at the power chords.'

As we drove on, I stared out of the window at the lion statues lining the river and then at the huge dome of Saint Paul's Cathedral. It's funny really – even though I'd lived in London for nearly my whole life, I'd never really seen it before then.

Miss Peters and Mr Wu were waiting for us outside the huge building hosting the furniture exhibition. Miss Peters was wearing another new scarf, one that looked surprisingly like a squirrel. Mr Wu was wearing his favourite pair of shorts, a very short bright red pair. The funniest thing though was that Mr Wu and Miss Peters were holding hands.

'Amy! Girls!' Miss Peters shrieked when we finally found a parking space and piled out. 'God is that you, Jade? You look so grown-up! And, Amy, you look wonderful. I'm so glad you made it. It hasn't been the same without you.'

She gave us each a perfumed hug.

'And who's this?' she said, raising an eyebrow at Ed.

'Hi, I'm Ed. I'd shake your hand, but I think

I'd better get this stuff unloaded before it starts to rain.'

'I see. Did you meet him at a salsa class, Amy?' Miss Peters cackled, and Grandma arched her usual eyebrow.

Stepping into the exhibition hall was like walking into Aladdin's cave. There were all these amazing colourful sculptures and pieces of furniture. Everything glittered or glinted or was brightly coloured. Even the people were sparkly: there were men with great big handlebar moustaches, women with spiky haircuts and silvery earrings and everyone was talking at once. The room was buzzing with excitement and I wished I could be a part of it, but I felt all tingly and nervous and my belly felt as if it was full of sea snakes.

I wasn't the only one who looked a bit sick. Jade had clammed up the moment we stepped into the exhibition hall. Grandma looked worried. Mum, however, was jumping around and arranging everything in a hundred different ways. She kept bossing Ed around while running around with her paintbrush. Our little booth kept getting turned upside down and back to front, and Mum kept adding little touches here and there. Finally Ed gave up and flopped on to the sofa. He pulled out a white handkerchief and waved it above his head. 'No more, no more,' he said.

Mum and Grandma stepped back and looked at our display and then at one another and nodded.

'It's perfect,' Mum declared.

We all huddled around to see it.

It felt as if all our stories had come to life. The patchwork couch and the rocking bear chair just begged to be touched. The chairs and table and trunk all shone with colour, the silvery touches catching the light. Ed had even scattered the floor with dry leaves and twigs and Mum had painted stars all over the walls of our booth. It was like a magical place you could only find if you crawled in through a special tree trunk.

'We have to win,' I whispered to Jade. 'We just have to win.'

But Jade didn't say anything. She just took my hand.

With all our pieces set up, we had time to watch everyone else. We saw people putting complicated metal displays together and arranging their furniture pieces into precarious towers. One woman had a bedroom made out of what looked like ice. Everything was hard and white and the walls were covered in mirrors. Above her booth she had a machine blowing out paper snowflakes. In the booth next to hers were huge dangling lamps that looked like alien spaceships, and across from that was a man who had made a wooden bath that looked like a boat. Everyone was talking, laughing and shouting at each other all at once. They all seemed to know one another.

'Colin, darling,' a woman in big black sunglasses was saying loudly, 'I just love how your style has evolved.'

It didn't take us long to make friends. Everyone wanted to know about the rocking bear chair. We were even invited along to see other people's pieces. It felt like the time we all went to the Little People's Conference. Everyone wanted to know everyone else there. Mum and Dad, and even me and Jade (because we were still little then), were just like everyone else, yet somehow I felt like I was in a room with the most special people ever.

I felt like I belonged to the most wonderful club in the world.

'I wish Dad could see this,' I whispered to Jade.

As the hustle and bustle started to fade, a man with a very bushy beard but no moustache appeared up high on a podium at the back of the hall. A second later his face appeared on two large television screens and a voice crackled out. All at once everyone's heads craned upwards.

'Welcome, exhibitors and guests, to Interior Art, London and the world's premier designer furnishings show.'

Everybody started clapping. The excitement was infectious.

'I hope you win, Amy,' Grandma said. 'I really do.' And she gently placed her hand on Mum's shoulder.

'Ladies and gentlemen,' the beardy-man's voice continued, 'while you have been putting the finishing touches to your exhibits, and having the opportunity to connect with one another, the other judges and I have been very busy.'

Jade looked over at me and shrugged and we looked back at the overhead screen.

'We have had a long, secret look at each and every one of your pieces,' he said, 'and I have to say, the standard of this year's show is very high indeed. The judges have greatly enjoyed seeing some very creative designs. But I'm afraid there can only be one winner and this year it is . . .'

Mum, Ed, Grandma, Jade and me all held our breath. I closed my eyes and thought about Harriet with her little coloured ribbons tied around the ends of her dreads and how Anna's lips always turned purple after eating grape lollipops. I thought of Mrs Mitchell and art class, but most of all I thought of home. Our shop with the sign Dad had painted and the little flat that we had all lived in. Jade tugged at my sleeve, and as I opened my eyes I saw the screen behind the man change. The word 'winner' flashed up in bright pink with the Interior Art logo. Then the microphone crackled and everyone started clapping. But I hadn't heard what he had said.

'Jade, Jade, who won? Who won?' I said, tugging at her sleeve. But Jade just stood there, her mouth going up and down like a goldfish's.

'Mum!?' I yelled, but she had been suddenly

surrounded by Grandma and Ed, Miss Peters and Mr Wu and they were all talking very fast. Then the big screen at the front changed again to show a woman's face. But it wasn't Mum's. It was the woman with the icy bedroom and snow blower. She was grinning from ear to ear, but I didn't understand why. She couldn't have won. She just couldn't have, because that meant we hadn't.

The microphone crackled to life again and the man with the beard said, 'We have the winner of this year's Interior Art with us now: Mildred-Anne Digby, with her snow-queen-inspired bedroom.'

'Wait – there's been a mistake! That's not right!' I shouted. But the room exploded into applause and my words were swallowed up.

Twenty-seven

Even when we went back to our display, I still couldn't believe it was true. While Mum and Ed started packing up the chairs and carrying out the couch, I kept waiting for someone – anyone – to run over and tell us there had been a huge mix-up. That the judges were secretly waiting for us backstage. But no one said anything, apart from Grandma who was trying to pretend everything was all right. She kept talking about how fabulously we had done and how much she liked Miss Peters' scarf, even though I could tell she didn't. Jade just stared at the floor and balled her hands into fists. She wouldn't look at me.

After Mum had loaded everything back into our truck, I sat in the middle of our empty booth, staring up into the painted stars. I felt if I just wished hard enough on them, I could make every-thing right.

'Come on, Sydney, we have to go,' Mum said, shaking my shoulder gently.

'If we set off now we can stop for chips,' Ed added.

But I knew if I could just stay put I could make everything all right.

'Let's just get out of here, all right?' Jade said, pushing me in the back.

But I shook my head and closed my eyes. I tried to summon all of Dad's magic, all of my shrinking techniques. I squeezed my hands and scrunched up my feet and held my breath. I kept chanting over and over in my head, '*I'm going home. I'm going home. I'm going home.*' Just when I thought I was about to pass out, I heard Miss Peters and Mr Wu. They were yelling for Mum in high excited voices. I opened my eyes to see them rush over.

'There's a woman over there who wants to talk to you,' Miss Peters said.

Mum shrugged. 'Another time. I really have to get these two home.'

'But, Amy, she wants to talk to you about your

furniture,' Miss Peters insisted as they dragged Mum and Ed away.

I looked Jade straight in the eye and grinned. 'I knew it had to be a mistake,' I said. Then I grabbed her arm and Grandma's too, and we all chased after them.

When we finally caught up with them a red-haired woman in a long green dress was deep in conversation with Mum and Ed. 'So tell me,' the woman was saying, 'what is the theme of your fascinating collection?'

'It's about memories,' Mum said. 'It's about taking precious things from the past and making something new.'

'Yes, I see that now,' said the woman, flicking her ringed finger through her hair. 'And with quite some style, if I may say so. It reminds me of a set from a fairy tale.'

Mum and Ed nodded politely, but I just wanted her to hurry up and tell us that there had been a huge mix-up and that we had really won.

'And it's exactly that connection that I'd like to talk to you about,' continued the woman. 'Theatre props and design!' she said grandly. 'You see, I'm the manager of a West End theatre company. And I'm always looking out for new designers. Making things for the theatre doesn't pay well, but it is a good way to get you some exposure. You do understand?'

'Uh-huh, uh-huh,' said Mum and Ed, nodding in unison as Miss Peters clapped her hands above her head excitedly. But this was wrong, all wrong. This woman had to be here to give us our prize, not offer Mum a job.

'Anyway, I assume you're on the Internet?'

Mum continued to stand there, just smiling up at the red-haired woman. She was probably as confused as I was.

'I mean, you do have a website?'

'Oh, a website. Er, yes, I mean, I could,' Mum said.

'Well, good, so I'll look you up, see what else you could offer me.'

Mum glanced at Ed.

'Um,' said Ed, 'actually we're just in the process of setting up our website. But if you give us your number, we'll let you know when it's ready.'

The woman nodded and rummaged in her huge

red velvet bag. Wordlessly she handed Ed a business card before floating off in a cloud of perfume.

'Oh my God, can you believe that?!' Miss Peters shrieked, flinging her arms around Mum's neck. 'Amy, I love this man,' and she pinched Ed's bum. 'We're just in the process of setting it up indeed. Could you *be* any smoother?'

'Well,' Ed said, laughing, 'I guess I'm the brains and Amy's the brawn.'

Mum elbowed him in the thigh.

'Only joking,' said Ed. 'Well, Amy, it looks as if we are going to have our work cut out for us when we get home to Portsmouth. We've got to design a website for one thing.'

Even though everyone was whooping and hugging one another, and Grandma gave Ed a little handshake, I felt frozen. This was all wrong. It couldn't be happening. Portsmouth. We were still going back to Portsmouth. It finally sank in.

'Hey, aren't you happy, honey-bun?' Mum asked me, her face all smiles. 'Time for a new start.'

I don't know what happened next. It was kind of like that time I was sick on Mrs Pervis, something just bubbled up from inside me. But it wasn't vomit, it was words. Hard, loud, screamed ones.

'I don't want a stupid new start. I want our old life back!'

I could feel people turning and staring, but I couldn't stop. I felt like I was growing bigger and bigger. All the things I wanted to say were making me swell like a toad. I felt that if I didn't get the words out I would explode.

'I want things to go back to how they were before we lost the shop. To before we knew Miss Peters and Mr Wu. To when I was little, when Dad was alive!'

But saying it out loud didn't help; it made me feel buzzy with anger. And I felt it happening again: the Wild Thing was taking over. I tried to do a shrinking exercise, but it was too powerful. The Wild Thing was pushing through my body. I felt filled with this animal fury. I had to get away to stop myself from hurting Mum or smashing things up. Mum looked at me, her face full of confusion, but I turned and ran. Ed and Mum started after me, but the crowd was in the way. People were finishing packing up. I weaved in and out of them until I couldn't hear Mum shouting my name any more. And before I knew it my feet had carried me away from my family, away from the exhibition, away from the icy-white snow-queen bedroom. Then I was outside, in the streets of London. Hard pavements, black taxis and red double-deckers. The hot press of a London crowd. I elbowed my way through them. Not thinking where I was going, just letting my feet take me further and further away. Before I knew it, I was far away from the exhibition centre and completely alone.

But by then I knew where I had to go.

Twenty-eight

London was much bigger than I remembered. And it was hard trying to find my way on my own. When I stopped running I found myself in a street I didn't know, surrounded by shops and buildings I had never seen before. I started to feel a bit scared. The Wild Thing had abandoned me again and I could feel bubbles of panic rising up in me. Had I really just left Mum and Jade and Grandma and Ed? Had we really not won the competition? Would we have to go back to Portsmouth for good?

But I reminded myself that I couldn't think about all that now because I had a mission. I was sure if I could get home, to my real home, to our flat, that everything would be OK. I didn't know how, but it would.

I needed to ask for directions, but the only person around was an old man sitting on a flattened-out cardboard box. A mess of dreadlocks poked out from his little grey bobble hat and greyhounds lay either side of him. They were making contented dog noises as he stroked their shiny coats.

Mum always said to be kind to the homeless. She bought the *Big Issue* and sometimes gave the seller a cup of coffee. But she also said never to talk to strangers. Adults were full of conflicting advice. To be honest, I was a little scared to ask him. But I also realized that I had no time to be scared. I had to get back home. I looked again at the greyhounds' soft faces.

'Excuse me,' I said, 'can you tell me the way to the nearest tube station?'

The dreadlocked man looked up from his dogs and pointed. 'Down this street, take a left and carry on walking and you'll find yourself there in no time.'

One of his dogs woofed in agreement.

I nodded a thank-you and headed down the road. Mum had made me memorize practically all the tube and train routes to Battersea in case I ever got lost. I wondered if she was worried about me now. I tried not to think about it. I was only one tube journey and then a train ride to Clapham Junction. From there I knew my way like the back of my hand.

At Waterloo station, I stuck the five-pound note Ed had given me for lunch into a ticket machine. Luckily I had been too caught up in the excitement of the show to get food. A couple of people gave me funny looks. I'm nearly ten but I still only look about eight. They must have thought I was too young to be getting the train on my own, so I made sure to find a family and tagged behind them. My fake-family had a mum carrying a huge tote bag with a picture of a fox riding a bicycle. It was one of the reasons I picked them. The bag kept sliding up and down her arm as she yanked a little boy behind her. He was halfway between deciding to throw a temper tantrum or falling asleep. The dad followed behind, keeping a close eye on both of them, so it was easy for me to fall in at the rear without arousing suspicion.

When we got on the train I made sure to get a seat next to them. The mum and dad seemed to be arguing about something that sounded like 'cheeses', so they never even glanced over at me. The little boy, after being ignored for stamping his feet, soon fell asleep. The dad scooped him up and the boy wrapped his chubby arms around his dad's shoulders. He looked so happy. I wondered if me and my dad had ever looked like that.

As I watched them get off at the next stop, a part of me thought about really going with them. Then the doors slid closed and they were gone forever. I moved up the carriage and sat next to an elderly woman with dyed lilac hair. She smelt of flowers and wet cigarettes and talked loudly on an old brick of a phone about all the people she knew who had died recently. I was really glad she was only my pretend family.

The moment I got off the train at Clapham Junction I started running. I couldn't wait to get to my real home. I had the key clasped tightly in my sweaty hand. It's funny – I'd never bothered carrying it around when I had lived in the flat, but I hadn't been asked to give it back when we had left and I had taken it with me to the competition for good luck. I couldn't wait to get back. But as I turned around the corner and saw it – the slanted red-brick roof, the big shop window – my heart stopped. The shop window was covered in newspapers. The gold lettering was gone. A 'For Rent' sign was up in my little window. And in the cool summer evening, out of the shadow of the doorway, stepped Grandma.

'Sydney Goodrow!' she shouted. 'Are you trying to kill me?'

I turned into a statue, unable to think what to do next.

'At my age,' my grandma went on, shaking her head, 'you could have given me a heart attack. Why, I could have just plain passed away on the spot when you disappeared like that.'

I tried to form words, but all that came out was snotty bubbles because I had been running so hard.

'Everyone's looking for you. Your mum and Ed went back to the truck. Jade and that woman in the ridiculous scarf are still searching the exhibition centre. But I had a feeling you might turn up here so I took a taxi.'

I expected Grandma to go on and give me a

huge lecture in the middle of the street. But she didn't. She just stepped aside.

'Well, go on then,' she said. 'I don't think there's anyone in.'

Inside, the flat felt completely changed. It wasn't just that it was empty. I had forgotten we had had to paint the walls plain white before we left, and without all our pictures the place wasn't as homely as I remembered it. All that was left of our time there were little indents in the carpet where our furniture used to be.

Grandma watched me from the doorway as I rushed tearfully into the kitchen. I was searching for the one sign that meant we had really belonged here. The marks on the door frame that had recorded Jade's and my birthday heights.

But they were painted over too. I ran my fingers over the place where they used to be, but I couldn't even feel any bumps or dents. It was smoothed over with new white gloss. Everything I'd had was gone.

'I painted over them, Sydney. Your mum couldn't do it. She couldn't bear to touch anything left by your father.'

I glared at my grandma and felt only pure hat-red. How dare she? I wanted to whirl my fists through the air and knock her face off. Instead I just screamed at her, 'You hated him!'

I had never screamed at Grandma before. But I had never felt so much anger. Maybe I was becom-ing the Wild Thing permanently, because at that moment I couldn't imagine what it was like to feel anything else.

Grandma didn't look at me like I was an unearthly Wild Thing. She just sighed, and for the first time that I could remember she looked like an old lady.

'Of course I didn't hate him,' she said. 'Your father was a wonderful man. But he was a dreamer, and that meant that sometimes your mum had to pick up the pieces.'

She leaned against the wall. 'You were probably too young to remember all the arguments.'

Now I thought about it I could remember Mum and Dad arguing. It was just that we never talked about our past any more. It was because we never talked about it that I was so scared I would forget. That I would forget the smell of Dad's hair, or the way he told stories like nobody else on the planet, and the way he made my mum so happy and so mad all at once. But most of all I was worried that we would all forget who we really were.

'This place was too full of memories,' Grandma said quietly. 'That's why I wanted your mum to leave.'

'But that's why we need to stay,' I said, and I realized I was crying. Not the kind of crying they do in films. No, it was the horrible red-faced snot-dripping-down-your-face kind of crying. The kind of crying that has you gulping for breath. The kind of crying that feels like it will never stop.

And that was when my grandma hugged me.

My grandma is not a touchy-feely kind of person. She would usually never risk getting tears, or mucus, or whatever other kind of horrible gunk was leaking out of me, on her carefully assembled outfit. So as she held me close, it made me cry more. I burrowed into her cashmere jumper until I couldn't see the old flat any more. All I knew was that my grandma was holding me tightly and stroking my hair.

'When your grandpa died, the only thing that

got me up in the morning,' she said softly, 'were the cats. They weren't even my cats. They were his. I used to argue with him that pets should be kept outside, not in. But afterwards I couldn't shut the door on them. I couldn't get rid of anything of his. I had a whole house full of his things. His old clothes, pictures, books, even his leftover medicines. I left all those chemist's bottles with his name printed on them in the bathroom cabinet for months.

'In the end, I knew I had to move away. And I just left it all there. All those things that had belonged to him. But that doesn't mean I've forgotten him, Sydney. Just because you move on, just because you leave stuff behind, it never means that you forget.'

As I pulled away from Grandma, I realized she was crying too.

'I took the cats though.' She sniffed. 'Stupid things just won't leave me alone.'

We stayed in the flat a little longer. I wanted to say a proper goodbye this time. I wanted to say goodbye to the shop, where Mum and me had spent so many Sundays painting together. I wanted to say goodbye to my old room, where I'd read books and decorated the walls with drawings and had sleepovers with Anna and Harriet. I wanted to say goodbye to the rooftop where me and Jade had watched the stars.

And lastly I wanted to say goodbye to Dad. Even though Grandma had said that I didn't have to. That moving away would never take away my memories. I felt I needed to say a goodbye anyway. So I whispered a shrinking mantra.

> *I never need to grow too far, or too tall.*
> *Keep me just as I am,*
> *Just perfectly small.*

Twenty-nine

The drive back to Portsmouth felt like the longest journey ever taken in the history of mankind. There were traffic jams and arguments, mostly about me running off. And then there were excited conversations about building websites, followed by more arguments about Mum needing to go back to her awful office job until she could make enough money to at least go part-time. And then there were a whole new lot of arguments about Ed's place in our lives. In the end I must have fallen asleep, because when I woke up I could smell the sea air of Portsmouth and it had turned dark enough to see the North Star over our house. The brightest star in the sky.

Jade and me curled up in bed together. I wasn't sure if it was because of the fire, or me running off, but it felt like it did before. Before Jade had turned into Dangerous Jade, before I had unleashed the Wild Thing, before we had moved here, and even before that. It felt like we were back to being sisters again.

'Did you really go all the way back to the flat?' Jade whispered.

I nodded and then we didn't talk for a while. I just lay there and smelt the clean bedding and the vanilla perfume Jade had worn that day.

'Tell me something about Dad,' I said after a long while.

'Which story do you want to hear?'

'No, tell me something *about* him.'

Jade sighed and rolled towards me and pulled the cover up over our heads.

'Do you remember how scary his "three-minute warnings" were? *If you're not both ready for school you're going to face all hell. This is your three-minute warning!*' Jade said in her best impression of Dad. 'I don't think I have ever been so scared to find out what would happen after three minutes. And do you remember that time when the car broke down because he hadn't put petrol in it? We had to push it that last bit home, and he bought us sweets so we wouldn't tell Mum. You ended up throwing up Skittles in this amazing rainbow vomit.' Jade laughed and then sniffed. I couldn't tell if she was crying. All I could see were the whites of her eyes.

'And do you remember that time . . .?'

But I had already fallen asleep.

Early the next morning, Jade was back in her own bed and the skies over Portsmouth were all grey and dark.

Mum had been in the kitchen making coffee and arguing with Grandma on the phone. I will never understand why they call each other just to fight. When Mum hung up the phone though, she turned on me.

'I didn't have the time to properly talk to you about what happened yesterday. And I don't have time now because I have to get ready for work,' she said, 'but I want you to know – when I get home there are going to be consequences, big consequences.'

I felt all the relief and happiness from last night slink away from me. After all, we were still in

Portsmouth. Mum still had to go back to her office job and our old life was still gone for good.

'I expect more from you, Sydney. After everything with your sister, I thought you were the good one. I thought you were grown-up enough . . .'

Mum pushed her hair back and started pacing, searching for the right words. I could see this was going to turn into an epic rant. I was in serious trouble. But I didn't care any more. The Wild Thing had abandoned me for good, and I just felt sad. Even though I had said goodbye to Dad, I still missed him.

'I had to go back. I had to go back for Dad,' I said in barely more than a whisper.

'Oh, Sydney!' cried my mum, all her anger gone, and she cradled me to her. She held me tight in her little arms.

'I was scared of forgetting him.'

'It doesn't matter how much changes, we don't forget the ones we love,' Mum said, stroking my hair. 'Nothing would have made him prouder than to watch you grow up.'

'No, it wouldn't,' I said, struggling away from her. 'He wanted me to stay little.'

Mum shook her head in disbelief.

'He wanted me to be like you and him,' I went on. 'So he taught me how to shrink.'

'You mean the games he played with you and Jade? Sydney! Your dad never meant it like that. He was so, so proud of both of you. He just never wanted you to feel wrong or out of place for having little parents. He wanted to make you two feel a part of something special.'

'But it worked. My shirts got bigger on me—'

'I switched your school shirts for some of Jade's and got her some new ones. You were getting too big for your old ones.'

It felt as if the ground was slipping away from me. Like I was tumbling, tumbling up into the sky, up into the stars and far away. Everything was a game. Just a game. But the funny thing was, I think a little part of me had always known I could never be like Mum and Dad, no matter how hard I tried.

'But I'm not special like Dad and you,' I finally said. 'I'm just ordinary.'

'Oh, honey-bun,' Mum said, brushing the hair away from my face. 'Being small was the least interesting, the least amazing thing about your dad. And, Sydney, you are so special for so many different reasons. You don't need to be anything other than who you are.'

Mum didn't hug me or start crying. She just looked at me as if I was the most magical, special thing in the world. Like a Fabergé egg or a new constellation or a hot little meteorite you could hold in the palm of your hand.

But as I looked at my mum, the bravest person I know, I just felt sad. 'Aren't you lonely? Being the only little person, without Dad?'

'How could I ever be lonely with my girls?'

I could feel tears bubbling up. But I was too old to let Mum see me cry so I kept sniffing and sniffing. Until Mum pulled me into another great big bear hug.

'You'll always be my little girl, no matter how big you get.'

And even though I was too big for her arms to go all the way around me and she had to stand on tippy-toes to let me put my head on her shoulder, it didn't seem to matter any more.

Then she said, 'OK, I still have a bit of time

before work, so you and Jade hurry up and get ready and meet me at the truck. I think it's time I took you somewhere.'

When we joined Mum outside, I half expected Ed to be waiting for us too. But he wasn't.

Mum must have guessed I was looking for him because she said, 'I think this is a trip just for the Goodrow girls.'

Then she started the engine and winked at Jade.

Mum put the truck in gear and we sped off. Past my school, past the arcade, even past the park me and Bobby had got lost in. And then up, up over the hill until we were above the city. I saw Portsmouth wrap around us, until it fell out of sight and there were only trees. Then, when I felt we couldn't get any higher, Mum stopped. She got out of the truck and beckoned for us to follow. So we followed, past some bushes to a clearing.

'This is Portsdown Hill, the very top of Portsmouth,' Mum said. 'Sometimes I like to come up here to think. Mostly it's when I'm thinking of your dad.'

Her eyes watered and she swallowed hard, gulping back air. She looked like Jade the time she ate a whole red chilli pepper. She took my hand gently and squeezed my fingers.

The three of us stood and stared out at the view before us. From up there I could see everything. My school, our neighbourhood, even the funfair, and beyond that the sea. It stretched out before us till it met the never-ending sky.

'Not exactly London, is it?' Jade said, punching my arm, her lightning-bolt earrings swaying in the wind.

Mum reached into her bag and pulled out the last three fortune cookies.

'I think it's time for some new fortunes,' she said.

Jade raised an eyebrow at me as she snapped open her cookie.

'*Time to set the world alight*,' she read.

'Yeah, maybe you should give that one to me. I think we've had quite enough fires set by you lately,' Mum commented.

Jade took another cookie, looking ever so slightly sheepish.

'*Life is about the people you meet*,' she read out. 'Who writes these things?'

Mum laughed. 'Shut up and eat your cookie.'

I thought about all the people we had met here. About Ed and his stupid dance moves and his wonderful breakfasts, and the way he made my mum giggle when she thought we weren't around. About Grandma, who I was only just getting to know, who was both really wise and yet absolutely ridiculous and just a little bit scary. And about Bobby, who had shown me the sea. I realized I didn't need to read my fortune, because it didn't matter any more. Things would keep changing, and maybe I wouldn't stay small. But I would never outgrow my mum, and I would never forget my dad.

In the early sunlight I watched our shadows stretch out across the hill and down over the city. Three giants standing together.

The End

Acknowledgements

Thank you to my parents, the true patrons of the arts. To Dad, my first editor. Mum, my cheerleader, and Ryan, whose one-syllable words of encouragement were not unappreciated. Also to my friends for providing the pints and long chats in the pub. Special thanks to Chris Dobson who read through many drafts and Rose Tomaszewska who championed my book. Big shout out to the whole team at Quercus and my editor Niamh Mulvey, who made this a much, much better book, and scared me senseless by telling me to make it twice as long! To my agent Hellie Ogden for her support, especially for the time she rang me from up a mountain. Sinéad Burke for her very insightful notes. Kristyna Litten for her gorgeous cover art. Jacqueline Wilson for her amazingly kind and supportive letter, which now hangs over my desk. And finally to the whole team at Blackwell's Portsmouth, who let me be their unofficial writer in residence.

If you enjoyed Sydney's story, here are some
of Amber Lee Dodd's recommendations
for other inspiring heroines, in fiction
and beyond . . .

DOLPHIN from *The Illustrated Mum*
by Jacqueline Wilson

Dolphin is a different kind of brave to your average hero. She doesn't fight witches or monsters or armies. Instead, she needs courage to deal with a difficult home situation, and sometimes that's when you need to be bravest.

GERDA from *The Snow Queen*
by Hans Christian Andersen

There are very few fairy tales in which the girl gets to be the hero. Actually, there are very few fairy tales where the girls aren't just married off to princes. So, *The Snow Queen* is the kind of fairy tale Sydney would love because Gerda gets to save the day. In this story, Gerda has to save her best friend Kai from the wicked Snow Queen. She must restore his good heart, which has been turned cruel by a cursed mirror shard.

MATILDA from *Matilda* by Roald Dahl

Matilda is a special kind of girl, not just because she discovers she has magical powers, but because she embraces a love of reading. Really, it's Matilda's love of books that gets her through some very tough and even dangerous situations.

FEO from *The Wolf Wilder*
by Katherine Rundell

Feo lives with her mum in the snowy forests of Russia, where she teaches wolves to be wild again. Not just any girl can work with wolves; you need to be brave and just a little bit wild yourself.

THE OVITZ FAMILY

Not heroines as such, but certainly heroic: the Ovitz family were a group of Romanian Jewish actors and musicians, several of whom were dwarfs who performed as the Lilliput Troupe. They survived the concentration camp Auschwitz through their commitment to one another and their unbreakable family bond. Our heroine Sydney is inspired by the Ovitz family at school, and I think we can all learn a lot from the family's strength and bravery.

And now for one of Sydney's gran's heroes …

CAROLINE HERSCHEL

Gran loves everything to do with science and the stars, and she is especially fond of Caroline's story. Born eight of ten children, Caroline was struck with typhus when she was little. As a result she only ever grew to 129 centimetres, barely taller than Sydney's mum. Caroline's mother was convinced her daughter would never marry, so she demanded Caroline be taught to be a house servant. Caroline's brother, the astronomer William Herschel, thought otherwise and made her his assistant. In 1786, she became the first woman to discover a comet and one of the first pioneering women astronomers.

We hope you enjoyed this list! Amber would love to hear about your favourite heroes and heroines. You can tweet them to her @AmberLeeDodd or send them via her website:

www.amberleedodd.com

AMBER LEE DODD was born and grew up on the island city of Portsmouth, where she rode the waltzers, swam in the winter sea and lost her wellies in the marshes.

Now she spends most of her time poking around second-hand and charity shops for fabulous old hats. That is, when she's not writing plays and stories.

Amber's plays have been performed at Chichester Festival Theatre, the New Theatre Royal and the Edinburgh Fringe. Her stories have been published around the world and broadcast on BBC Radio 4. *We Are Giants* is her first book.